I0687087

Wrong Line, Right Connection

by

Karina Bartow

Wrong Line, Right Connection

Cover Art by *Kim Mendoza*

The Wild Rose Press, Inc.
PO Box 708
Adams Basin, NY 14410-0708
Visit us at www.thewildrosepress.com

Publishing History
First Edition, 2022
Trade Paperback ISBN 978-1-5092-4259-7
Digital ISBN 978-1-5092-4260-3

Published in the United States of America

When the motel lit up a third time, she dropped the preamble. "I'm sorry, Mr. Stentz. I'll get it right this time."

"No problem, but now that I think about it, you can give me the number, anyhow. That way, I won't have to trouble you if I need to make another call during my stay."

She did her best to conceal her humiliation while she recited it. She didn't cry often, but to her alarm, a tear traced down her cheek. With him living out of the state, they probably would never cross paths, but discouragement washed over her. She blew her chance, if she had one to blow in the first place.

"Thank you, miss." His chivalry didn't crack, a sign of what a nice fellow he must be, given what she put him through. "Since I have you again, I wanted to ask if you'd like to go to dinner with me tonight? I was hoping someone could show me the sights before I head north. Plus I'd like to find out if you're a better date than you are an operator."

Dedication

In Heartfelt Memory of
Grandma Mabel & Grampy Roy

To Jennifer Wilson
Thank you for "connecting" me to the "right" story!

Prologue

July 1960

Mabel Banks sat on her suitcase, smooshing it down to accommodate her beloved mink coat. She never wished to be fifteen pounds heavier until now. She resisted all those pies and cakes over the years, and for what? To keep her girlish figure? Her fur coat hid her figure, and most people didn't notice how many pounds were underneath it. Why hadn't she discovered that sooner?

If she'd planned to stay, she would've marched into the kitchen and made a gelatin mold right then. For once, sweets couldn't persuade her, and neither could that man. She allowed him to manipulate her for five long years, but deep inside, she expected it to lead to this. When his number of apologies matched his number of indiscretions, she could tolerate it. She even cleaned out his precious chicken coops day after day, regardless of the toll it took on her sore back and the filth it left under her once-gorgeous nails. Nowadays, his harsh speech and misdeeds prevailed more than ever, as his remorse dwindled. Maybe he'd sprout a conscience once he had to glove up and start scooping.

She stood back up to evaluate her work. The mink now resembled the dead animal from which it was made. She opted to give up on compressing it into the

1

bag, but she refused to leave it behind. She could imagine the pleased grin that would spread over his face if he found it deserted. He gave it to her for their wedding, the only good she reaped from the day. She once regarded it as a symbol of his love for her and desire to make her happy, but she grew to believe otherwise. In truth, he used it as leverage, her incentive to keep up the veneer of wedded bliss and ignore the crummy way he treated her.

With no other choice, she wrapped the coat around her and braved the ninety-three-degree heat boiling through Irvington, Kentucky. A taxicab honked its horn outside the ranch house, signaling the end of her real-life nightmare. She put on her hat atop her red curls and latched the suitcase. She shook her head in disbelief that the single bag carried all the belongings the cheapskate—whose last name oozed with irony—allowed her to own. More than any of them, including the mink, her memories box held priceless value, and she clutched it close to her, separate from her other possessions. At first, guilt pierced her for taking it into a new home and a new marriage, but in retrospect, she couldn't have survived this without it.

She waltzed out the door with both arms full, not giving the slightest look back at the place for closure. Like a wounded soldier, she didn't yearn to take in the battlefield one last time. Carried by her red heels, she focused straight ahead and pranced to the car awaiting her. She loaded her luggage into the cab and lifted her foot to get into it, but the crunch of gravel in the distance halted her steps. She grimaced and peered at the pickup truck of one of her husband's associates trotting down the driveway. Being too late to make her escape undetected, she rushed over to the truck.

To her relief, Bobby, the farmer's son, handled the deliveries today.

"Hi, Mrs. Banks." The nineteen-year-old gave her a friendly smile when he hopped out and strode back toward the bed. "Ned ordered another dozen."

Her husband never informed her of his purchases, even if he commissioned her to tend to them. "Oh, did he?"

"Yep. I need you to sign." He handed her a notepad and pen, regarding her attire. "Are you cold?"

She kept her reply simple. "Not at the moment."

She wrote her married name one last time to avert confusion and an awkward conversation. He grabbed hold of the boxes one by one and placed them beside the coop per her instructions. The contents clucked the whole time, prompting a genuine smile to cross her lips for a change.

Bobby gave her another once-over but kept a grin plastered on his face. "I see you're headed out. Would you like some help putting them inside?"

"No, Ned will do it after work."

She let out a giggle after he drove away, taking off her wedding band and leaving it on top of one of the boxes.

Chapter One

June 1964

Mabel strolled out of the movie theater, observing her fifteen-year-old niece, Beverly. The love-struck teenager bid *adieu* to her first boyfriend, Harold, moments earlier, but she maintained the smitten radiance surrounding her all evening. Her aunt allowed her to bask in her youthful bliss while she gleaned similar joy from her chocolate-covered frozen banana sold at the concessions stand. She figured she ought to dim her glow, however, before she dropped her back off with Millie, her sister and Beverly's strict mother.

"Didn't that film have a happy ending?"

Beverly's smile and dopey gaze didn't falter. "Yeah, it did."

She wrapped an arm around her and laughed. "I can tell what an impression it made on you."

"What do you mean?"

"It's about the most famous shipwreck in history, Bev! Over a thousand people died." She could've admitted that the movie's main character survived, but she wanted to find out if the girl noticed.

She didn't. "Oh, I thought so, but I didn't want to argue with you."

"Right, and it has nothing to do with the fact that your feature presentation didn't involve the movie I paid for you and what's-his-name to see."

She slowed her pace for a moment and offered a coy smile. "It entertained us."

"I gathered that."

"Come on, Aunt Mabel. You've fallen in love, a few times, in fact."

"I sure have, and you know what I've learned from those experiences? That when a man can't keep his lips off you, he's trying to stop you from talking. When he can't keep his hands off you, he's trying to stop you from getting away."

Bev rolled her eyes. "Well, you may have gone through that, but it doesn't mean I will."

Mabel nodded, unable to refute it, but it pleased her to note the flushness of the girl's hot cheeks had faded. She didn't need Millie accusing her of being a bad chaperone.

The bus parked at the stop before they made it there, but the long line awaiting it gave them time to catch up and join the other riders. She polished off the last of her treat before they boarded, while Bev finished her soda.

The two found a bench a few rows behind the driver, and some other stragglers stepped onto the bus before it could depart. The doors closed, and they began the journey home. She gazed out the window at Louisville's lights, always captivated by the excitement of night life in the city. Everything awakened as Ned's chicken coop—if he could still manage it without her—and the rest of Irvington tuckered out.

She suppressed a chuckle over the memory of her former life and her departure from it four years ago. Like she'd wanted, her sudden exodus made her unsuspecting ex furious. To her disappointment, he didn't try to convince her to return...but she wouldn't have, anyhow. She emerged from the marriage with too many emotional and physical scars to let him sweet-talk her into giving him another chance.

Bev's voice jolted her out of her nostalgia. "Have you given up on love?"

Truth be told, she contemplated that question countless times, even in the months before she left Ned. She still couldn't settle on an answer, but she wouldn't let it on to her niece. "Of course not. I have love in my life. I have you guys and Duke, and I love Evelyn on her good days."

"I'm talking about loving a man."

"What do you call Duke?"

"A dog. Wouldn't you?"

Mabel shrugged. "I feed him, clean up his messes, and stroke his ego. I don't see much of a difference."

Bev shook her head with a grin, but she didn't concede, proving she inherited some of her aunt's tenacity. "I remember when you and Uncle Ned were happy."

She never failed to cringe inside whenever Bev referred to him as her uncle, but she repressed her bitterness. The girl had been five at their wedding, where she filled the role of flower girl, so she recalled her times with them through the eyes of a naïve child. Plus Ned treated her well through the years, buying her a doll once and bringing home an ice cream for her when she visited. Her age didn't allow her to notice his lack of care for Mabel.

Having overcome her animosity enough not to point out his many flaws, she chose not to dispute

Bev's statement. "We can't depend on other people to make us happy."

"Sure, but we shouldn't count on them to hurt us and push them away, either." She gazed over with a somber expression that pierced Mabel.

Nonetheless, she kept her humor intact. "I don't push anyone away. My boss wishes I did. He's written me up three times in two months for flirting with customers."

"Flirting with men over the phone won't lead to a real relationship, and you know it. That's why you do it."

Her insight impressed her aunt. "Leave the old woman wisdom to me, will you? I'm the one who's pushing the half-century mark."

She would've liked for her niece to tell her forty-one wasn't old, but the teenager made no such assurance. Even so, Bev complied, dropping the subject for the rest of the journey. They both rode to the Springhill stop, where Mabel escorted Bev to her parents' house. Since she talked to Millie before the movie, she didn't stay long. She needed to catch the last bus of the night to get home to Brownsboro. On occasions like this, having a car of her own would've made it more convenient, but she didn't regret her decision not to learn how to drive. In her opinion, legs cost far less and offered much more reliability.

Their conversation stuck with her as she rode alone. She didn't like to contemplate her love life, much less talk about it. Either direction she could go— seeking another *man of her dreams* or accepting a future alone—opened up countless good and bad possibilities. She longed to be Bev's age again, without the experience to warn her of consequences. Some considered it wisdom, but she regarded it as invisible handcuffs others slapped on her. Sad to say, she'd acquired multiple sets by now.

Arriving at her stop, she stood and brushed off her blue dress, even if it didn't need it. She supposed she did it to shed the feelings the evening threw at her. Stepping off the bus, she headed left and passed the three townhouses before hers. Well, it technically belonged to Evelyn, but her friend always created a homey atmosphere for her.

She grew up around Evelyn, and by coincidence, they crossed paths the day she returned to Louisville. Mabel stopped at the grocery store on her way to Millie's, and the two ended up checking out at the same time. Her suitcase and mink lying in the cart made her plight rather obvious, and Evelyn offered her a place to live without hesitation. Being seventy-eight at the time, she confessed she wouldn't mind having an extra person to help manage the house.

Each passing year added more duties for Mabel to perform, and in recent months, she had to care for Evelyn. The older woman could still get around, but she needed help cooking and remembering her medicine. Without any of Evelyn's children around to call, Mabel took on the roles as they became needed, never drawing anyone's attention to it.

Evelyn sat in the living room, reading a book with Duke at her feet when Mabel entered. The sight surprised Mabel, given her friend always retreated to bed before this hour.

She spotted the mystery novel in her hands. "Another case keeping you up late again, Detective?"

Her eyes didn't leave the page. "Yes, I have to know if I'm right about the killer. How'd your night go with the love birds?"

"Nobody's pregnant, so I guess I did my job." She sat down in her usual armchair. "Leave it to a square like me."

"Who called you a square?"

"That niece of mine. She seems convinced I'm a habit away from joining a nunnery."

That took Evelyn's attention off her book. "You? Oh, if only she'd known you as long as I have. At her age, you didn't consider a movie entertaining enough to deem it a suitable date."

"Well, they were silent back then."

"They beat what we had in my day, my dear." She winked. "What did the kids use to call you back then?"

She gave way to a smirk. "Merry Time Mabel."

"That's it. See, Bev doesn't realize what she missed."

"What she missed? What do you mean by that? I still like to have fun."

"Yeah, but your idea of fun now is beating me at cards or tossing the tennis ball to Duke at the park."

Upon hearing his name, along with the words *ball* and *park,* the blond Scottish terrier opened his eyes and scampered over to Mabel. His brown eyes pled with her to follow through on the remark.

"Maybe tomorrow." She rubbed his ears to seal the promise. "Speaking of which, I'd better get up to bed. Don't stay up too much longer, or else I'll tell you the ending."

"If you do, I'll take Bev's side and drop you off at that nunnery before she can."

She snickered at the threat as she climbed the narrow staircase up to her second-story bedroom. Once inside, she took off her hat and heels, after which she changed into her pink nightgown. She folded back her sheets and began to sit down, but the memories box called to her from its spot on her dresser. A few months having passed since she peeked inside it, she indulged her urge in an effort to reflect on the girl she used to be.

Despite how many times she opened the lid, the delicate rosebud on top of the collection never failed to mesmerize her. The sight always took her back to the day she received it in the spring of 1946.

****

Mabel sat beside the hotel pool, flipping through a magazine she bought in the gift shop. She relished in the solitude, given her parents and sister stuck nearby since they arrived in Chicago four days ago. At twenty-three, she didn't jump at the idea of going on a family vacation, considering most of her peers took trips with either friends or their own spouses and children. Plus she left home three years before and didn't enjoy having to abide by her folks' rules again or sharing the bathroom with Millie.

With the temperatures still in the low seventies, a cool breeze bit through the air, which discouraged guests from taking a dip. Alone on the patio, she basked in the delight of wearing her black and white polka dot swimsuit beyond her father's notice. While she skimmed through an article on summer fashions, the door behind her opened. She pivoted, expecting one of her family members to join her, but instead found the hotel's handsome groundskeeper.

She spotted him when they checked in Friday

morning and instant tingles prickled her when he smiled as he walked past. To her disappointment, she didn't notice him after that, but she later assumed he didn't work on the weekend. At last, he surfaced again, without her watchful dad and nosey mom and sister to interfere.

The light brown-haired man did a double-take upon catching sight of her, and the same smile crept up on his face. He carried a box of chlorine tablets along with a pair of gloves and knelt down to grab the pool skimmer. He extended it to retrieve the container floating across the water, before he spoke up, his voice deep but kind.

"You're the first person I've seen out here this year."

She became aware of her bathing suit all of a sudden, and to her surprise, her cheeks warmed. Normally, she would've glowed over an attractive man catching her in the alluring garment, but this stranger gave her pause. She couldn't determine why, but regardless, she retrieved her cover-up. "Yeah, well, I suppose I have a case of spring fever."

"You're not alone. This winter dragged on. Are you from the Midwest?"

"No, Louisville, but we suffered through a colder one than usual. Even the whiskey farmers took pity on their produce and carted it inside. If you ask me, I think that suited their own comfort more than anything."

He chuckled. "Sounds like a nice way to stay warm."

She watched him open the floater and drop in the tablets, before releasing it back into the water. "Why do you need to do that if no one's swimming?"

"If we didn't start early, it would look like a swamp in June. How long are you staying with us?"

"Till Friday. My father is attending a business convention, and my mom and sister coerced me to join them."

He sauntered toward her. "I'm glad they did, Miss…"

"Jennings. Mabel Jennings."

"Clark Russell. I'll see you around." He removed his glove to shake her hand. After he let it go, he produced a pink rosebud from his back pocket. "Here's something to brighten your room. I know our decorating department needs some fresh designs."

****

Mabel still grinned at the thought of his smooth gesture.

Interrupting her reverie, one of the old floorboards squeaked, and she spotted Evelyn standing in the doorway. She nodded to the rose. "Does it still have its smell?"

She drew the bud up to her nose. To her disappointment, no scent wafted up from it, but she resisted admitting it. "A little bit."

"He chose well."

"Yes, he did. I couldn't believe it when he confessed he spotted me out there beforehand and snuck it away when he decided to approach me. That moment just seemed so natural and effortless. Everything did with him."

"That's how you know when love is real; it doesn't require a whole lot of fuss. Things fall into place, even beyond your notice."

Mabel murmured a word of agreement, before she

switched topics. "Did you finish your book?"

"No, I ran out of steam and skipped to the last page. I guessed right that the guy's best friend did it."

"Well done. I expected it to be the nephew."

Evelyn waved off the notion. "Nah, he didn't have the guts or the intellect."

Mabel giggled at her analysis, and the two wished each other a good night. Her gaze drifted back to the rosebud, which she twirled between her fingers. She'd forever cherish it and the love it set in motion, a love that ran deeper than she could've imagined.

When she returned it to its place in the memories box, a twinge ached in her heart, certain no other love would grace her path like that again.

****

Mabel hopped off the bus on Sixth Street and pranced down to the eleven-story building where she worked. She'd spent two stints as an operator for the telephone company, the first when she graduated from high school. That time lasted for over five years and ended with her on good terms with her employer, despite her occasional flirting and eavesdropping on customers. When she returned to Louisville, she didn't hesitate to go in and ask for a job, even if her former boss retired during her thirteen-year-long absence. Not to her surprise, they were hiring, and the supervisor welcomed having a veteran who didn't need training.

She trotted up to the third floor and into the locker room, where she stowed away her black patent leather pocketbook. She checked her watch, rushing to get to her station before Lorna arrived. The twenty-one-year-old irritated her from the moment they met. The girl was nice enough, but she treated Mabel like a dinosaur.

She voiced her supposed amazement of Mabel's stamina and her ability to read the small digits on the switchboard. Her coworkers kept telling her Lorna meant them as compliments, but she didn't buy it. In her opinion, the brownnoser wanted Mabel to retire so the boss would pay more attention to her.

She let out a groan upon meeting the blonde in the doorway.

"Good morning, Mabel. Did you enjoy your weekend?"

"I did." She considered telling her she wasted hours knitting and drinking prune juice to complete Lorna's archaic view of her, but she decided against it. "How did yours go?"

"It was lovely, thank you. We're busy putting the final touches on the wedding, so it didn't leave much time for leisure. I'm sure you remember how it goes."

"Yeah, I think I can fetch back that far."

The girl chuckled. "Rodney found the chance to buy my wedding present. He gave it to me Saturday."

Mabel leaned in to admire the silver chain she held up from her neck, from which a small sapphire pendant hung. She deemed it too small for such a special occasion, but she wouldn't pop her balloon. "Very pretty."

She started to resume her trek to the switchboard room, but Lorna stopped her again. "Will you be joining us on our big day? I believe you're the last one to RSVP."

She gritted her teeth, the question needling her for months. Evelyn encouraged her to *be the bigger person* and go, but she couldn't stand the idea of being regarded as the old hag there. She assumed the bride's family and friends would act just like her, and if so, she'd rather attend a funeral in hopes the people there would treat her like her actual age.

"I'm sorry I didn't tell you sooner, but I can't make it. I meet with my knitting group, and it's my turn to provide the prune juice."

Lorna's eyes sparkled more than ever, telling Mabel she didn't want her there any more than Mabel wanted to go. "Oh, sounds like you'll have a full day. We understand."

Instead of taking offense, she walked off, pleased to have the conversation behind her. When she entered the switchboard room, the three girls who worked the night shift sat at their stations, their tired posture revealing their need for relief. She could relate, having suffered through six months on nights when the company first hired her. Still, she mused at how much easier this generation had it, with the advanced system and the fact that most people could now dial directly. In her day, they needed at least a dozen operators at night to cover the heavy load.

When Mabel made it to her station, her coworker, Wendy, occupied her seat, busy with a caller. Mabel waited for her to transfer the person to the desired line before she spoke.

"Busy evening?"

"Yes, especially for a Sunday. A half hour didn't go by between calls."

Again, Mabel found humor in the younger staff's perspective. "Well, it's the first weekend of summer. The kids have to strategize a hundred days' worth of mischief and figure out whose parents they should hit up for bail money."

Wendy smiled. "Sounds like you're speaking from experience."

Mabel shrugged and gave her a wink. "I might be."

The light above the jack that connected the ongoing call faded out, indicating both parties hung up their receivers. Wendy plucked out the cord and put it back into its original jack before notating the call's duration. Once finished, she stood to allow Mabel to take her place and handed off the headset before the two wished each other a good day.

The first hour passed without much activity, like always, but the board picked up after the workday started. At this point, Mabel recognized most of her customers by their number and could anticipate most of their requests. A call from one of the motels rang in before long, another indication of summer's arrival. She straightened her back to become more professional, having to prepare to speak with anyone.

"Good morning. To whom am I speaking?"

"Mr. Roy Stentz." He spelled his last name for her in a deep voice. She'd encountered many men with masculine voices, but for some reason, this one hit the button inside her that triggered an automatic, insuppressible smile. His tone boomed but not in an offsetting way. Rather, she detected a gentleness, though she didn't have any valid reason to make such an assumption. Lost in it, she didn't even start scribing his name until he said the final letter, but she figured out the rest.

"What may I do for you, sir?"

"I'm from Pennsylvania, and I'm here to tour the steel warehouse. I misplaced my paperwork and need the phone number."

"Of course, Mr. Stentz. Give me a moment while I find that." In truth, she memorized the extension by heart, having forwarded hundreds of calls to them in her career. She didn't want to send Roy Stentz away just yet, however. "May I ask where you live in Pennsylvania?"

"A small town called Coatesville, about an hour west of Philadelphia."

"And you work in the city?"

"No, we have a factory there, believe it or not. We're working on two hundred years in business and hope to double that by upgrading the equipment, like they've switched to here."

She wondered why he'd travel all the way to Louisville instead of going to a closer city like Pittsburgh, considering its prominence in the steel industry. She didn't care enough about it to ask for details but would've liked to converse with him on another topic. She resisted, realizing she'd better wrap up the chit-chat. Experience taught her men grew irritated after two unnecessary questions, especially on a business call.

"I have the number here, sir, but why don't I patch you right through to them? It'll save you a step."

"I appreciate that. Thank you, ma'am."

"It's Mabel, I mean Miss Jennings...no, Mabel Jennings." She never disclosed her name unless someone asked her for it, and she regretted doing so after she flubbed the simple statement.

He didn't seem to mind, the tone in his voice suggesting a smile. "Thanks, Mabel Jennings."

Her cheeks warm, she hooked into the factory's line and announced Roy's name to the person who answered. She depressed the knob in front of her to cut off her end of the exchange. At times like this, she longed for the obsolete system she used to operate, when she could eavesdrop. The topic of their discussion didn't interest her in the least, but she would've enjoyed listening to his deep voice for a little longer.

Georgette, the woman beside her, raised an eyebrow. "I know that face."

"What face?"

"The face you get when you hear low octaves. Nobody's frazzled you like this before. A guy has to be really something to leave Mabel Jennings tongue-tied."

She opened her mouth to refute it, but the pencil in her hand drew her attention elsewhere. "Oh no, I forgot to record the time I transferred him."

"And the time the call ended." Georgette nodded toward the unlit lamp on the board.

She took out the line in haste and estimated the times. "See what you made me do."

"Me? I'm not the right gender to put you in a tizzy."

Moments after she finished her scribbling, the motel's line rang again. Georgette reached for it, teasing, but allowed Mabel to take it. She inhaled a deep breath to regain her composure.

"Good morning. To whom am I speaking?"

"Roy Stentz, Miss Jennings. I'm sorry, but you connected me with the wrong line. The hardware company answered instead of the warehouse."

Her cheeks burned redder by the minute. "I apologize for that. They're positioned next to each other. I'll connect you again."

Cramped by embarrassment, she switched around

the wires and announced him once more to the second recipient. Right away, she wrote down the time, refusing to even glance at Georgette, whose playful eyes she sensed on her. The call, again, ended before a minute had elapsed, and as she grasped the trunk, she realized she still placed it in the wrong line.

When the motel lit up a third time, she dropped the preamble. "I'm sorry, Mr. Stentz. I'll get it right this time."

"No problem, but now that I think about it, you can give me the number, anyhow. That way, I won't have to trouble you if I need to make another call during my stay."

She did her best to conceal her humiliation while she recited it. She didn't cry often, but to her alarm, a tear traced down her cheek. With him living out of the state, they probably would never cross paths, but discouragement washed over her. She blew her chance, if she had one to blow in the first place.

"Thank you, miss." His chivalry didn't crack, a sign of what a nice fellow he must be, given what she put him through. "Since I have you again, I wanted to ask if you'd like to go to dinner with me tonight? I was hoping someone could show me the sights before I head north. Plus I'd like to find out if you're a better date than you are an operator."

Chapter Two

Mabel spritzed on a touch of perfume, still reeling from the way this date was set in motion. The instant she hung up with Roy, she regretted accepting his invitation, given how little she could discern about him. She didn't have a clue as to his identity and even needed him to wear a blue carnation so she could recognize him. He could be married and seeking a fun trip without his wife. Or he could've brought her with him but claimed he had to go on a business dinner. Either way, she didn't want to get mixed up in that.

She debated whether or not to call the factory and have the secretary give him the message that she couldn't make it, but she reckoned it'd be a pretty low move. Just as he could be a shady character, he could also be a great guy, and she didn't want to embarrass him like that. Thus she opted to follow through on her word. She just hoped the restaurant would boast a large enough crowd to discourage him from any poor intentions he may have.

She put on a pair of clip-on earrings, and her gaze drifted to her memories box, its lid still open from the night before. She stepped over to close it, but she spotted the embossed napkin she saved from her first date with Clark. She snickered inside, remembering how that, too, rooted from a haphazard start.

****

Mabel climbed into the back seat of her dad's green sedan to go to dinner, but she froze when she heard him holler, "Good night, nurse!"

"What's the matter, Rusty?" her mom cried.

"The spare's gone flat now."

Mabel shuddered at the nightmare this would unleash. They ran over a nail at a rest stop on their drive from Louisville, forcing him to put on the spare. Her mom begged him to buy a replacement, but he insisted on waiting until they returned home.

As Mabel anticipated, her mom couldn't suppress her nagging. "I told you…"

"Enough, Sarah."

Since they couldn't go anywhere soon, Mabel decided not to bother cramming into the small back seat. Millie stepped out, too, and the two of them watched their parents bicker, making the girls exchange knowing smiles. Their dad crouched down to better inspect the leak, and Mabel glanced away for a moment. In that instant, she caught sight of Clark, who, to her surprise, peered in her direction at the same time. They locked eyes, but reluctant to stare, she scanned her other surroundings. His gaze must have lingered, with him meandering over.

He approached her father. "Is something wrong with your car, sir?"

"Oh, it's just a flat. I reckon I'll need to call for a tow."

"Let me check it first." He knelt to the ground and ran his fingers over the tire. He stopped when he made it to the eleven o'clock position and rubbed his index finger on it. "Here it is, and it isn't very big. I have a patch that'll take care of it."

"I don't want to put you to any trouble."

"You aren't. I'll go get it from my car, and you guys will be good to go in ten minutes tops."

He headed to the back lot, where she guessed the employees parked. Millie gave her a grin and a wink, despite Mabel's not sharing their meeting earlier that day. Clark's handsome features could make a half-blind woman giddy.

He returned and retreated to his stance beside the wheel, and her dad joined him. He applied the patch and sealed it. The older man circled his thumb around it once he finished, as if to ensure the quality of the job. Seeming to approve, he rose to his feet and slipped out his wallet.

"How much do I owe you, son?"

Clark stood. "Is dinner with your daughter too high a price?"

****

She didn't expect tonight to lead to the bond she and Clark developed, but she supposed she shouldn't give up on something based on its rocky beginning. Still, she had to tiptoe over more than her own misgivings. Her roommate didn't approve of her choice to accompany him, convinced he'd be a criminal. Mabel kept wondering if her primping would be in vain, afraid Evelyn would trap her in the house.

Evelyn scowled from her seat as Mabel touched up her lipstick in the foyer. "I cannot believe you agreed to go out with an out-of-towner you've spoken to once."

"We talked three times, as a matter of fact."

"Yeah, and who's to say he doesn't plan to lock you up somewhere to pay you back for the trouble you caused him?"

"Who's to say he won't join me?"

The older woman harrumphed. "I don't understand what's taken away your good sense. You never do anything this foolish."

Mabel couldn't argue with her, but she wouldn't confess the reservations she had, either. She also couldn't share the conclusion she arrived at when questioning her reason for obliging him. As much as she hated to accept it, she realized Bev's accusation that she avoided establishing a real relationship persuaded her.

Overnight, she pondered what awaited her in life. She didn't like the younger generation treating her like an old maid, but she realized she earned the label in many ways. At forty-one, she hoped half of her life still lay ahead of her, so why not enjoy it? It may or may not include a man, but she didn't want to rule it out.

Her conversation with Lorna reinforced her resolve, as she didn't like the thought of her days of romance being no more than a memory. She didn't foresee another Clark in her future—and didn't want to stumble across another Ned—but someone else could make her happy, couldn't he? Based on his voice alone, she presumed Roy Stentz could.

She could imagine the rebukes her friend would throw out if she explained it all, so she acted casual. "Didn't you accuse me of turning into a bore last night?"

"I'd rather live with a bore than a fool." She shook her head and sauntered into the kitchen.

Mabel grinned and dropped her lipstick into her clutch before waltzing out the door. She arranged to meet him at six-thirty, and her watch told her she had twenty minutes to get there. With the restaurant she chose just three blocks down their street, she'd arrive in plenty of time.

Ambling along, her questions about Roy continued to persist, and she slowed her pace a couple of times due to her doubts. She revisited their introduction more than once in her mind, trying to analyze his character without her emotions toying with her. Quite a few men flirted with her through the years, and the majority made their intentions clear from the start. She reciprocated on many occasions, but she never put too much stock in the admiration. They would've hit on anyone who answered in a feminine voice.

With Roy, on the other hand, he remained professional during the first two calls. If anything, she manifested ulterior motives by prolonging their chat. For his part, he didn't seem interested in her until he became more acquainted with her qualities…even in an unflattering way. That didn't strike her as a guy desperate for any kind of woman's company.

She formed a plan to evaluate Mr. Stentz before she committed to dining with him to appease her sense of reason. As she approached the restaurant, she unpinned the carnation from her blouse with a grin. She strolled up the ramp attached to the white house-turned-eatery and entered the lobby, where she spotted a tall man wearing a blue carnation on his lapel. His blue eyes glowed with kindness under his thick-rimmed glasses, and he'd slicked back his dirty blond hair. Like his voice, his appearance gave her a thrill, but she determined not to let her attraction sway her.

Since she didn't frequent the place, the staff didn't recognize her, which facilitated her scheme.

"How many are in your party, ma'am?" the maître d' asked her.

"Two, but I'm waiting on my husband to park the car. We'd like to sit on the patio, if it's available."

"A couple tables out there opened up a few minutes ago. I'll make sure one's ready."

Mabel thanked her, delighted she left them alone. She avoided engaging with Roy right away in an effort at subtlety, but she couldn't wait too long. "Sounds like a busy night for a Monday."

"Hard to beat this weather."

She nodded, trying to conceal her thrill over hearing his voice in person. "You come here often?"

"No, this is my first time. I'm here on business from Pennsylvania."

"Oh, that's nice. Did your wife join you?" She wished she'd asked this on the phone and averted the whole matter.

"No, I'm not married." He gave her the response she sought.

She couldn't formulate a suitable reply, now aware of what a tricky debacle she created. Silent moments ticked by, until the maître d' returned and took it out of her control.

"We have a two-top open for you. If you follow me, I can show your husband back once he gets here."

A smile crossed Roy's lips, telling her he'd caught on to her game. "I wonder what's taking him so long."

"What gave me away?"

"Your voice."

She dropped her gaze, shaking her head at her own stupidity. When she conjured up the nerve, she told the puzzled hostess, "I'm trying to convince him I'm a better operator than a date."

"You're getting close," Roy teased.

Mabel put her hand over her eyes in jest. Neither she nor Roy said a word while they followed the hostess to their table. Her humiliation rivaled the embarrassment she endured at her dinner with Clark. She slouched in her seat, just like she did as she sat beside her intruding father.

****

Mabel assumed her face had blushed to a deeper shade of red than her hair. Her dad agreed to let Clark take her to dinner, but on the condition the rest of the family accompany them. Worse still, he insisted they share a corner booth, with her parents and Millie sitting between them. Determined to ignore them, she talked across the table, but they kept interrupting. She suspected her dad gave her mom and sister a handbook on the art of pestering.

"How long have you lived in Chicago?" she asked him.

"My whole life. I grew up in the suburbs but moved downtown after I graduated from high school."

Her father latched right onto that. "Have you ever met up with any gangsters?"

She rolled her eyes, unable to believe he'd address such a subject.

"No, I was too young to understand what was going on at the height of those times. My dad claims to have seen a crew of them once at a bar. Those days have passed. They take better care now to keep their operations underground than they did back then."

They fell silent again, with the clatter of their utensils serving as their only discussion. She ran through topics that wouldn't elicit feedback from her family, but every one failed. Despite how much it annoyed her, Clark impressed her with the way he handled it, never making an unkind face or sharp remark. She, on the contrary, couldn't stop rolling her eyes.

After she finished eating, she asked him where she'd find the restrooms, and he gave her directions. To her relief, her mother and Millie didn't follow her, so she could let out a few groans of frustration in the vacant room. She lingered a bit, primping her dress and adjusting her pearl necklace. In the end, she wondered if Clark would even notice her efforts amidst the many distractions at the table.

She opened the door with a sigh and began her trek back, but she halted her steps when she spotted Clark standing by the coat rack. He raised a finger up to his mouth, grinning.

He held out the crook of his arm for her to take. "What do you say we let them entertain each other for a while?"

"Sure. Why waste their talents on us?"

****

While Mabel skimmed her menu, she hoped they could overcome the awkward circumstances in a similar way. In the meantime, she continued to sneak glances at Roy. He still remained quiet, but he didn't manifest any signs of irritation. Like on the phone, he displayed a calm, patient manner, the upward turn of his lips indicating admiration. His motives still baffled her, given he couldn't consider her much more than a kook.

"If you like Dutch food, people rave about their special smearcase." She didn't like the fancy cottage cheese when she ordered it on her first visit there, but she didn't care for many Dutch dishes.

He shook his head. "I don't have a very refined palette, despite my wife's best efforts. As hard as she tried, she couldn't persuade me to eat anything more exotic than frog legs."

While pleased to learn they shared similar tastes, she almost sprang to her feet the instant he mentioned his wife. "But you said—"

"She passed five years ago from cancer." He returned his attention to his menu and cracked a smile. "That's what you get for coming here incognito."

She sank a bit more into her chair, embarrassed. "Well, I didn't know much more about you than your voice."

"And I didn't know much more about you than your absent-mindedness."

"And yet, here we are." She chuckled, before acknowledging his statement, "I'm sorry you lost your wife. My husband passed at a young age, too. He suffered a brain aneurism when he was twenty-eight."

He extended his condolences, and the two resumed their quests for the right entrée. She didn't bother to qualify her statement about her husband's death, often omitting her second marriage from her narrative. She didn't deem it anyone's business, and many still found it unacceptable for a woman to end a marriage. Besides, she hadn't considered Ned a husband in a long time. She viewed him more as a tyrannical landlord with whom she shared a last name for five awful years. She refused to say the word *divorcee*, preferring the term *survivor* with regard to the outcome of their relationship.

A waitress approached their table and took their orders, with both requesting the Kentucky country ham meal. After the girl left, Mabel peered around the yard, its beauty accentuated by the perfect June evening. The gentle breeze rustled through the tall oak trees and the tassels hanging from the umbrella above them. She refrained from marveling at the scene for too long, not wanting to appear like a rude companion.

Instead of hastening their retreat to small talk, she decided to throw another test at him. "So, why didn't it occur to you I might be married?"

"Well, you don't hide your emotions too well, so I figured I'd be able to tell if you considered my invitation improper."

"Is that your kind way of telling me I'm too big a ditz to pull off a crafty affair?"

He took a sip of his martini. "Maybe."

The wry comment would've infuriated her if anyone else uttered it, but she snickered at how it sounded when he said it. "If I weren't such a lady, I'd teach you otherwise."

He yielded to a burst of laughter. "Did you and your husband get to start a family?"

"No, we didn't have the chance." Like she always did when the subject arose, she strived to remain expressionless and numb the pain it inflicted on her. "Do you have children?"

"A son, Gregory, but he's out and on his own now. He headed off to Texas not long after he graduated from high school. This spring, he married a girl he met there the day he moved into his apartment. They're both too young in my opinion, but they're older than my wife and I were on our wedding day. Funny how things like that catch up with you."

"The kids don't have the maturity we did back then. My niece is fifteen, and she's not close to being as prepared for life as I was at her age." She drank some of her martini, reflecting. "Then again, I suppose our parents said the same thing about us."

"Mine did. They had three kids at the age I was when Gregory came, and my mother acted like I was a child raising a child. I reckon I'll be in her position in a year or two."

"I'm sure my mom would've acted like that with me, but she wanted a grandchild from the instant we said *I do*. She and my sister even set up the family cradle before we returned from our honeymoon." She shook her head but didn't disclose how much she liked the sight of it, in wait of a little occupant. In the end, Millie used it for Bev without Mabel ever having the opportunity.

She welcomed the return of their waiter with their food, which diverted the conversation away from children. They shifted to the typical subjects of work and home life. They'd both lived in the same general area since childhood and worked just a few different jobs. He started at the steel factory the same year she landed her first job as an operator. Since he didn't take the hiatus she did, he could retire in the next few years.

"How do you plan to spend your freedom?"

"I haven't given it much thought, to be honest. I guess I'll visit my son more, but I don't plan to relocate down there. I like the seasons, and Coatesville is home."

"I agree, but I've always wanted to explore the whole country. Staying in one little town seems like going on an African safari just to see a warthog."

"Everybody has their own prerogative," he stated in a kind manner, but she could sense he didn't share her aspirations.

The server ventured back over to take their empty plates away and offer them dessert. Mabel—who'd stuck to the resolution she adopted about sweets the day she left Ned—spoke up without hesitation. After a moment, she slowed her speech as she realized they never discussed splitting the bill. Should she presume a man who didn't know what she looked like an hour ago would buy her dinner, much less a dessert?

She found a polite yet independent way to clear up the confusion. "Please, add a piece of chocolate cake to my check."

"Oh, I'm sorry, ma'am, but I put you two together. I assumed…"

"You understood correctly, miss. Excuse her confusion." He shot across an impish grin at her and ordered a slice of apple pie.

Once the girl retreated to the kitchen, Mabel acknowledged his generosity, "Thank you. I didn't know if I'd proven to be a good enough date."

"You're not bad, considering our rocky start." He winked. "After all, I'm the one who imposed on your evening."

The remark reminded her of Bev's taunts. "Some might call it a long overdue imposition."

"What do you do when you aren't connecting people to the wrong lines?" Again, the left-handed compliment sounded endearing from him.

"I live with an older friend who I've known most of my life, so a lot of my free time goes to helping out around the house without her realizing how much of it I do. She's a bit stubborn."

"So, did she rub off on you or you on her?"

"A little of both, I suppose. You can't believe everything you read about us southern belles. We're not the dopey damsels in distress, in pantaloons with parasols over our shoulders." She shook her head, unable to fathom living in such an era. "What do you do when you're not asking out scatterbrained operators?"

"For the record, this is a first for me, and not just with a *scatterbrained operator*, as you put it. I haven't gone out with a woman since I courted my wife." His claim took her aback. "But to answer your question, I play the drums. I learned as a kid and joined a band in high school, but we parted ways once we started our own lives and families. I even sold my set to buy my wife's engagement ring. After she passed, though, I bought a new one and convinced a few of my buddies to return to music. We're thinking we might call ourselves Garage of Grandpas."

She laughed. "It makes more sense than that insect band from England who has the girls going wild."

"We do our hair better, too."

Their treats arrived and broke up the pop culture talk, making Mabel's mind circle back to his admission to this being his first date since he lost his wife. While she chewed, she wondered why he chose to take such a step with her. Did he consider her a safe candidate, given he wouldn't have to see her again after he skipped town? Did his hometown lack a good selection of women, so he took the first one he spoke to here?

By the time she polished off her dessert, she couldn't suppress her curiosity any longer. "How'd I earn the honor of being your dinner companion? You can't claim it was my alluring figure."

He grinned, pausing for a moment. Afterward, his posture relaxed, showing her he trusted her enough to get candid. "Well, I haven't smiled a great deal in a long time. My son's even suggested my facial muscles have forgotten how to. Of all times, I should've been grimacing in disgust this morning when you gave me such a run-around, but I couldn't wipe the smile off my face. I figured if you could bring that out of me by doing anything but trying, I ought to give you a chance."

****

Mabel didn't realize how nervous she'd been until after Roy's admission about her ability to make him smile. The compliment both touched and freed her, as it told her he liked her for who she was even without her trying to impress him. Few ever showed such admiration for her, and instead, she concluded her personality didn't mix well with most people's. She didn't put on a pretense, which didn't win her favor with those who did. She appreciated having someone like him admire that quality in her.

Staying true to that, she didn't take the kind words as an invitation to hone her comedic skills but enjoyed the opportunity to converse without worrying she'd offend him. Ned, who everybody liked, used to discourage her from expressing many of her feelings because he might lose friends. In contrast, Roy didn't display any such discomfort, his smile growing wider with the evening's progression. She deemed it an accomplishment in light of his confession.

When he rose to go to the restroom, she reflected

some more on his candor, still surprised by what he'd shared with a relative stranger. Then again, she recalled how much Clark revealed to her during their stroll in Chicago.

****

Mabel and Clark scooted out of the diner, a few feet between them. With other guys, she would've taken his distance to imply his lack of interest in her, but she perceived the opposite from him. She'd gone with boys who hastened the relationship, which only hurried it to its end. She didn't expect anything long-term with him, but to her surprise, she welcomed the change of pace.

Without discussion, they veered in the direction opposite the side where her family sat, avoiding their watchful eyes. They kept quiet for a few paces down the street, making her wonder why they escaped to continue doing what they'd engaged in all night. At the same time, the silence didn't bother her but offered contentment.

Clark leaned a little closer to her and exercised his newfound free speech. "Your family's something else."

"If I hadn't known that before, I would've now." She shook her head. "I must admit, I wouldn't want any other. They didn't need to try too hard to convince me to join them."

"I'm glad you did," he expressed for the second time that day. His green eyes locked with her blue ones, and they drifted toward each other.

"Me, too. Does your family still live nearby?"

"My mom and aunt do. They're the ones who raised me. My dad's a general in the military, so he's come and gone for my entire life. We could've followed him like most families, but my parents decided staying

put would give my brother and me stability. They were right in that regard, but we also lost the chance to get close to our father."

"That's a major sacrifice."

"I don't know if I could make it, having experienced the other side of it. As matters turned out, I didn't have to. I was born with a heart murmur, which doesn't affect my everyday routine but disqualified me to serve. Dad didn't take that very well, especially since the war started the year before I turned eighteen. He doesn't call me often, and Mom doesn't tell me when he's visiting anymore. He deems me the wimpy son. Every time I do have contact with him, he makes some sarcastic remark about my gardening, as he calls it."

"I'm sorry to hear that. From the little I've observed, he's missing out." She summoned the nerve to take his hand, though she typically waited for the guy to make the first move.

"Thanks. Your dad's given us a hassle tonight, but you should appreciate how much he values you. You may just think he protects you because you're his daughter, but blood doesn't guarantee love for everyone."

****

Mabel didn't understand what she did with Clark or Roy to prompt them to confide in her, but regardless, she appreciated meriting someone's trust. When Roy returned to the table, they prolonged their date by ordering an after-dessert decaf coffee. They took the hint to leave after they finished, when their waitress offered to take their mugs from them. He extended the crook of his arm to her, an unexpected pleasure, and they weaved their way around the tables scattered through the yard. The maître d' winked at them as they exited the lobby, seeming to surmise the night improved after she seated them.

"I'll accompany you to your car," he offered once they shuffled onto the sidewalk.

"Thank you, but I don't drive. My house is just a ten minutes' walk."

"You don't drive at all?" he asked, his voice suggesting astonishment.

"Nope, and it isn't because I'm a woman. I don't trust a mobile other than the ones under me. In a few years, I'm hoping I can upgrade to a couple of newer models."

"We can shop for some together." He let her go, but she could sense his reluctance. "Could I give you a ride home?"

His sweet eyes pleaded with her to accept, but she doubted Evelyn would approve. As much as she scolded Mabel for trusting a stranger to take her to dinner, she wouldn't appreciate her leading him to the house. Given how long Evelyn owned the place, Mabel couldn't make such a presumptuous choice.

Before she could decline, a familiar voice rang out from behind her. "Mabel?"

She spun around and beheld her roommate. "What are you doing here, Evelyn?"

The woman's steps grew shorter with each pace. Where it'd taken Mabel ten minutes to make it there, it no doubt took her double, at least. "Well, you've been gone so long, I began to worry. I almost called the police."

Mabel rushed to her side, putting an arm around her. "You should've called for an ambulance to pick you up, while you were at it."

Roy crossed to her other side. "Let's take a seat on the bench."

They assisted her to it, where Mabel also sat down and monitored her while she caught her breath. Once she recovered, she scanned Roy from head to toe. "You aren't as scary as I pictured."

"Well, you're feistier than I anticipated."

She beamed with delight. "I guess we underestimated each other."

"This goes without saying, but Evelyn, this is Roy. Roy, my roommate, Evelyn." The two shook hands, after which Mabel patted her friend on the shoulder. "Are you sure you didn't dart over here to snatch him from me?"

Her eyes twinkled, and she nudged her. "You carried on and on about his deep voice. Can you blame me for wanting to indulge my ears?"

Mabel put her head into her hands to conceal her embarrassment. When she ventured a peek at Roy, his amused expression warmed her heart.

Touching her further, he crouched down to their level. "Would you ladies give me the pleasure of driving you both home?"

Evelyn gave her a teasing wink. "I'd appreciate it, but Mabel may want the exercise."

"Did I mention how subtle she is?" Mabel asked Roy.

After another moment, they headed for the parking lot, and he led them to his bright red pickup truck. Mabel cringed inside, with it reminding her of Ned's beloved vehicle he used around the farm. Nonetheless, she climbed in and scooted to the middle of the seat, offering Evelyn a hand as Roy helped her. She settled in and thanked him before he shut the door, aiming a smile of approval at Mabel.

She guided him to the townhouse, which was a straight trek that only took three minutes. He rounded the truck so he could aid them in getting out, which prompted Evelyn to invite him to visit for a bit. He agreed but told them he couldn't stay out too late due to his early morning ahead.

Evelyn waved off Mabel's support as they walked into the foyer. Despite the older woman's stubbornness, Mabel insisted on retrieving a glass of water for her to drink. She offered Roy one, as well, which he accepted. When she emerged from the kitchen, she found him studying the pictures on the mantel, including her and Clark's wedding photo. She froze for a second, somewhat uncomfortable. Considering she already made reference to her first husband, she reckoned she had nothing to hide…except, of course, for her other marriage.

He sat down after examining the row. "You both were beautiful brides."

"Vincent and I don't compare to Clark and Mabel. Then again, they could afford the big to-do. We couldn't manage much more than the license."

"When did you marry?"

"September, 1902. Not the Depression, but not prosperous, either," Evelyn said.

"And what year did you and Clark wed, Mabel?"

"Forty-seven. When did you and…" She hastened to direct the conversation away from her past but regretted it upon realizing he never mentioned his wife's name.

"Heidi and I were married in forty-two. I proposed three weeks after we met, and to my surprise, she accepted."

"Were you headed to the battlefield?" Evelyn asked what Mabel wondered.

"No, I didn't go to war because my father died when I was a kid, and I had to care for my mom. Heidi lived in Philadelphia, and a mutual friend introduced us at a party. I watched all the guys flirting with her, so I figured I needed to make my move quick. We used to joke that we rushed to the altar because I hated having to drive into the city. I'll admit, I don't enjoy the traffic there, but she always made it worthwhile."

Listening to him, Mabel didn't wince with threads of jealousy like she once did when a date spoke of another woman. Rather, she admired his enduring devotion and could relate to it because of her attachment to Clark.

Unaware of her lack of envy, he seemed to want to dismiss the topic. "Enough about me. How did you two get acquainted?"

"Mabel's mom and I lived next door to each other before she was married. She watched my son for me once in a while, so I babysat her children when needed. I took Mabel under my wing after she lost both her folks. I'm so thankful I ran into her the day she escaped Irvington."

Mabel drew a deep breath, but it didn't prevent the inevitable.

"Irvington?" Roy questioned.

"Yes, the pesky little town where No-Good Ned dragged her," Evelyn explained.

"My ex-husband." Mabel straightened her back,

uncomfortable. She took advantage of his empty glass. "Would you like some more water?"

"No, thank you. I'm afraid I have to go. I enjoyed meeting you both."

Mabel's heart sank as he stood and shook Evelyn's hand. As he strolled toward her, she swallowed hard and endeavored to conceal her dismay. She assumed the mention of her divorce sent him scrambling, uneager to get mixed up with a twice-married woman. She and Evelyn didn't get into many spats despite their strong personalities, but she foresaw one tonight.

In a last-ditch effort to salvage his opinion of her, she escorted him to the door.

"I appreciate you allowing me to show you a bit of our city. I hope it didn't disappoint."

"I must admit I'd like to see some more, but I have the whole week. You gave me a nice head start. I enjoyed it."

"Me, too." She forced a smile, although she ached with despair over not having another chance to see him.

He put on his hat as he stepped onto the threshold. "Oh, I almost forgot to ask for your phone number. I'd ring up the operator, but I don't have a great deal of trust in the telephone company these days."

Chapter Three

Mabel awoke with a smile on her face, remembering several of her dreams that featured Roy's voice. A part of her wondered if she dreamed the whole day yesterday, since Roy's repeated acts of kindness seemed too good to have happened in a twelve-hour period. She'd made enemies with people in a lot shorter time span and for much less significant misunderstandings, so she marveled at the privilege to be on the opposite side for a change.

She rose a few minutes earlier than her typical time, so she used her extra moments to tidy up her room. She finally closed her memories box as she should've before, and she repositioned the photo of Clark and her beside it. Taken soon after their honeymoon, her favorite snapshot captured so many of the qualities she treasured in him. She sat on his lap at a friend's house during just an ordinary visit, but his loving eyes twinkled with the same genial nature he manifested the week they met.

****

Mabel didn't speak on the way back to the hotel, humiliated by her father's behavior. When she and Clark didn't return to the table right away, her dad hunted them down outside and interrupted Clark's narrative about his family. He behaved like a gentleman when her dad intruded on them, but he didn't stick around for long after they made it back to the eatery. Though he used his upcoming work day as his excuse, she believed he didn't care to play a part of the circus in which Dad acted as the ringleader. She couldn't blame him for it. Her father treated them like schoolchildren on a field trip, instead of dignifying them as adults on a date.

She sulked for most of the next day. She didn't go to breakfast with her mom and Millie or accompany them shopping, either. Rather, she stayed holed up in the room, unable to stomach the prospect of running into Clark.

Millie and Mom returned mid-afternoon, and she continued to give them the silent treatment, although they didn't bear any responsibility in this. She watched them carry in their bags of purchases and fought a sting of jealousy. Her mother's eyes darted over at her with insistence, which didn't help Mabel's mood.

"Will you please take a break from your pouting, and go down to get the last bag out of the cab? The driver's still running the meter. Give him an extra dollar for a tip, and you can keep the change." She handed her a ten.

Mabel never declined a bribe, so she sauntered out and took the stairs to the lobby. The taxi waited right outside the entrance, and she ducked her head into the back seat to retrieve the bag. Exchanging the money with the driver, she spun on her heel to retreat inside, until she caught sight of a familiar—handsome—figure approaching her.

Clark grinned at her. "Hey, you. I've been looking by the pool for you all day. I see you did some shopping?"

"No, my mom and sister did. I needed a bit of solitude after last night."

He stuffed his hands in his pockets, a twinkle of mischief in his eyes. "Did I annoy you that much?"

"No, not at all. You prevented me from suffering a nervous breakdown. I owe you an apology for how my father put such a tight leash on us," she told him.

"Don't worry about it. Like I told you, I find it refreshing when someone fawns over his family like that. Besides, it reinforces what a special person you are. I might not know you too well yet, but I understand why he wants to keep you close."

His words sent warm tingles down her spine. "Thank you. For what it's worth, I think he likes you."

"Does he like me enough to trust me to take you out on my own tonight?"

"I think the problem is he doesn't trust me enough to let you." She laughed.

He gave a shrug. "Then, I suppose I'll have to ask to tag along again "

****

Mabel noticed that the photo didn't evoke the usual ache inside her, and the longer she peered at Clark's eyes, the more they reminded her of Roy's. The notion took her aback, and she dismissed it from her thoughts as soon as it formed. She couldn't let her nostalgia distort her view of the present.

After getting dressed, she waltzed down the staircase and into the kitchen. "Morning, Evelyn."

"Aren't you shining as bright as a June rose?"

"Yes, thanks to Roy's open-mindedness. He let you and your blabbermouth off the hook."

Evelyn squinted, puzzled. "What did I blab?"

"My second marriage."

"Why would you hide that?" she asked.

"You know how people react when they find out I divorced Ned."

"And you know I keep telling you not to care what others say. You had to get away from that monster before he took you to the butcher along with the chickens."

Mabel finished buttering two slices of bread and set them in the toaster. "Don't bring up the farm at mealtime. I'm just happy it didn't ruin Roy's perception of me."

"Technically, he didn't hear you walked out on Ned. Even if he had, wouldn't you rather he realize it now and have the opportunity to accept you as you are than learn he's a jerk later? Mabel Jennings doesn't camouflage who she is to fit in with anybody."

She grinned and rubbed Evelyn's shoulder, grateful for the reminder. "No, she doesn't."

"Besides, it'd do a man good to understand you won't tolerate him treating you like an animal."

"Unless the animal is Duke. He's pampered like his namesake." She ambled over to the dog's dish and filled it before sitting down with her own breakfast. "I can't tell you why I panicked inside the way I did. I didn't expect to see him again, anyhow."

"Would you have gone in the first place if you had?"

She failed to respond, chewing her toast. She didn't mean to be rude, but she didn't have an answer. In fact, she debated the same matter overnight. Roy relieved her when he didn't write her off because of her past, but his request for her number planted a knot of fear inside her. True, she wanted to continue their rapport, but the prospect daunted her once it became attainable. Bev's words on the bus continued to taunt her, but she would never confess how well the girl had pegged her.

She also couldn't decide what she wanted out of this relationship. She experienced the heartache of finding and losing love in just days with Clark, so did she really want to repeat that? Her despondency as Roy stood to leave surprised her, with it revealing how fond she'd grown of him after a few hours. If she spent more time with him, how could she expect anything besides a lonely outcome by the week's end?

During her ride to work, she reasoned she should view it as a break from her typical, dull routine. Since her divorce, she didn't engage with many people on a social basis, least of all men. A far cry from the girl she used to be, she supposed she deserved a couple of fun nights, even if it didn't go any further than that. Plus her maturity would guard her from getting too attached like she did all those years ago.

She spotted Lorna the instant she entered the locker room, but the usual dread didn't drench her. Instead, she approached her without hesitation.

"How's the bride-to-be?"

Lorna paused before replying, as if waiting for another bride-to-be to respond. "I'm well, thank you. Like I told my mom last night, I can't promise I'll live till Saturday. I've been breaking my back to finish our centerpieces for the reception. How anybody can stand to get married more than once, I'll never be able to fathom."

"Me, neither." Mabel found gratification in her choice not to divulge her past to her young colleague.

"I'm sure everything will turn out beautiful."

"I hope so. Thanks a bunch for asking." She embraced her.

Mabel struggled to conceal her chagrin, wishing she hadn't allowed her tough exterior to soften. She broke away in mere seconds, but the minute she encountered Georgette wearing a devilish grin, she braced for another round of aggravation.

Her coworker almost sang her question. "How'd your evening go?"

She attempted not to play into the goading. "Fine, and yours?"

Georgette crossed her arms. "For goodness' sake, Mabel. You can't convince me the caller who had you bubbling with glee all day long just gave you a *fine* time."

"Why not? What makes you so certain he didn't end up being a pot-bellied loser?"

She gave her a pointed look. "I don't think a pot-bellied loser would put you in such a good mood that you'd voluntarily talk to Lorna."

Mabel closed her locker and made for the switchboard. "All right, I'll trust your assessment of my behavior."

More calls lit up the board than usual for a Tuesday morning due to the influx of summer tourists. Among them, Mabel connected a woman to Fountaine Ferry, the local amusement park, to ask for the price of admission for her family. She answered such curiosities when she could but deflected this one. Bev was a toddler on Mabel's last visit, so she couldn't guess how much the cost had inflated by now.

Not long into the mother's conversation with the

ticket office, the line of Roy's motel illuminated. The duty to answer it fell on unoccupied Georgette, but Mabel didn't care to follow the rules in this instance.

"Keep tabs on the ticket office." She slid over the slip so she could notate when the call ended.

Georgette jabbed her with her elbow. "Aren't we eager to talk to the pot-bellied loser?"

Mabel sneered at her, punching her jack into the line. In the event someone other than Roy responded, she resorted to her standard greeting. "Hello. To whom am I speaking?"

"Mr. Stentz. To whom am I speaking?" His voice let on his impish motives.

"Ms. Jennings. I believe we became acquainted yesterday."

"That's correct, if I'm not mistaken. I look forward to pursuing that further."

"I do, too." With Georgette watching her, Mabel shifted her gaze away. "For the time being, with whom may I connect you?"

"The steel warehouse, please."

"Didn't I give you their number?" she asked.

"Yes, but dialing it doesn't entertain me as much as you do. I enjoy the suspense you add to it."

She beamed with delight. "Haha, Mr. Stentz. I'm sorry to tell you, but I've grown too accustomed to your charisma for it to beguile me today."

"Then I guess I need to work on it." She could envision him winking when he said it.

"I reckon you should."

"Before you transfer me, have you thought about what you'd like to do tonight?"

Mabel glanced around to make sure her boss

remained in his office. Meanwhile, she noticed the call to the ticket office concluded, and she motioned the message to eavesdropping Georgette. "Well, it depends on what you'd like to see. To get the full Louisville experience, you'd probably want to go downtown at some point. We could go to…"

To Mabel's alarm, Georgette didn't follow her signal, too enthralled with the date planning.

She pointed to the line. "Fountaine Ferry."

Roy interpreted her words to be directed to him. "I passed signs for that on my way into town, and it intrigued me. I haven't visited an amusement park since my boy was in elementary school. I wouldn't mind spending a few hours there."

"I haven't gone in a while, either." She considered her hiatus from the place an accomplishment. As much as she loved thrills, she didn't need roller coasters to satisfy that longing. She wanted to find a way out of the notion, but his eagerness refrained her. "Should be fun."

"I'll say. Thanks for suggesting it. Would you like to meet me there, or could I give you a lift?"

Seeing as he already knew where she lived and she'd ruled out the possibility of him being a psychopath, she welcomed a break from the bus. "You can pick me up if you want to."

"It'd be my pleasure."

****

Scouring through her wardrobe, Mabel couldn't decide what to wear for the evening. Experience taught her skirts and dresses didn't mix well with so-called amusement rides, which played into her dislike of them. She owned one pair of slacks, but she didn't consider them suitable for most occasions, especially in the presence of a man. The young crowd called it progressive to start dressing like men, but she considered it a descent into a classless society. Besides, she wore them every day on the farm, so they didn't evoke good memories.

She opted for her yellow summer dress, deciding its flowy mid-length skirt would provide comfort without getting in the way. Moments after she put it on and smoothed out its loose wrinkles, Evelyn hollered that she had a phone call. She anticipated it'd be Roy canceling, and she raised her defenses in an effort to avoid disappointment.

Evelyn grinned when she handed the phone to her, and from it, Mabel surmised her plans remained intact. Unlike the previous night, the older woman welcomed the prospect of them getting together this evening.

She always had to resist the urge to continue with her usual introduction from work. "Hello?"

"If it isn't my lovesick aunt." Bev giggled.

"If it isn't my pesky niece."

"According to Evelyn, you listened to your *pesky niece* and snagged a new beau because of it. No need to thank me."

She lifted her eyebrow at Evelyn. "No need to gloat, either. Since you started it, though, do you realize now that my relationships over the phone can lead to something more?"

"Sure, when you follow my advice. So, where does he live?"

She ground her teeth at the question, aware of the trap awaiting her. "He's from Pennsylvania. He came here for work."

"Of course he did. Now I understand why you're going out with him—it won't go anywhere. How foolish of me to think I made headway with you."

With no time to waste, Mabel didn't argue with her. "Sorry to let you down, kid. Why'd you call, anyhow?"

"Mom and I wondered if you could go with me to Harold's baseball game Saturday?"

She hadn't started making her weekend agenda, but she didn't care to include a high school athletic event if she could help it. "Can't one of your parents take you?"

"No, they have to attend Dad's business luncheon. If Roy's still around, he could join us."

She chuckled inside over the girl's bait, but she didn't bite this time. To her relief, the ring of the doorbell gave her a way out of the conversation. "We'll talk about it later. He just arrived to pick me up. Have a good night, honey."

"You, too. Enjoy Fountaine Ferry."

Hanging up the receiver, she shifted toward Evelyn. "Did you have to tell her everything?"

"I needed to explain why I'd like her input on my love life."

She shook her head with a grin, grabbing her purse on her way out of the house. Roy rounded the truck to open the passenger's side for her, demonstrating his chivalrous side yet again. They both ended up at the door at the same moment.

He grabbed the handle and extended his other hand to her. "Have we met before, miss?"

Her joviality made it easy for her to spring up into the seat. "I'm not sure, but I recognize your voice."

After he climbed inside, she directed him on the

best route to their destination, hoping she remembered the details. Once on the main stretch, they chatted about their day. Mabel asked various questions concerning his work and the decisions he intended to make during his visit. She didn't understand a lot of what he explained regarding the machinery he inspected, but she tried to stay involved in the discussion. More than anything, her ears picked up his remarks about his to-do list awaiting him at home, and she hated how the simple words pricked at her heart.

Her memory didn't disappoint, and they arrived at the park with no trouble. The ornate entrance sparkled as bright as ever. She always considered it better suited for a glamorous theater than an amusement park. As they strolled through it, they passed several families departing, finished with their day. She wondered if any of them included the mom who called the station and set their date into motion.

She observed a couple of Black families among them, a new sight because of the park's longtime practice of segregation. After years of protests, Blacks and whites could access the whole place beginning that season. Having lived in the south for her whole life, she grew up accustomed to such policies and always accepted them without question. Nowadays, she wished she'd given it more reflection, particularly when she noticed the happy faces the newfound freedom promoted.

Due to the later hour, just one party stood in front of them in line. As they waited, Mabel took out her wallet, still not wanting to presume Roy's intentions. He spotted it right away and waved it aside.

"Why would I invite you and expect you to pay?

What kind of gentleman do you think I am?"

"I haven't figured that out yet. The other guys who flirt with me at work don't seem to be gentlemen at all."

"I guess I'm a rare breed." He winked. "How many times have you gone out with fellows like that?"

"Never. I hang up the instant they ask me whether or not I have a life insurance policy."

He responded with a loud laugh before they stepped up to the window. He purchased their admission along with a bundle of tickets for rides. The gesture alarmed her, having wished he shared her aversion to them. She determined to keep a positive outlook and allow him to enjoy the night. She could persuade him to use them all on his own.

Neither of them ate yet, so they agreed to stop at the first food stand along their path. They both selected fried favorites—a corn dog for her and an order of hushpuppies for him. For dessert, they split a funnel cake, both chuckling over the juvenile meal. While munching on the sugary treat, she noted Roy staring through her, quiet, igniting her insecurities. Did she bore him? Was he longing for his late wife?

After a few seconds, she chose to take a risk and address it. "Has my luster worn off already?"

His eyes slid over, bamboozled, but he seemed to understand her drift an instant later. "Oh, no. I'm sorry to give you that impression. I'm watching the ring toss game behind you. I've always done pretty well at those, but everyone who's played since we sat down here has lost."

"You ought to go back there and teach them a lesson."

He winked, letting on that he shared the notion.

Although they didn't discuss it further, they headed that way once they finished eating. The bounce in his stride tickled her. He approached the attendant and passed him a dime, which afforded him three rings to throw at the line of soda bottles. His first attempts missed by mere centimeters, the third ricocheting off one of the necks.

Roy handed over a second coin and another when that round proved unsuccessful. He forked out half a dollar before he began to scrutinize the plastic circle.

"Say, this is barely big enough to fit on them."

"It adds to the challenge," the teenage boy behind the stand remarked.

"No, it adds to your profit," he accused. "I've played this at numerous carnivals and have never seen them use a ring this small."

"Carnivals leave town within a week. We stay open all summer. We can't give away our prizes. You understand how businesses run."

Roy wagged his finger at the kid. "Yes, I sure do, and I can also spot a con from a mile away."

If she hadn't liked him so much, Mabel would've pointed out that it took him more than a dozen attempts to detect the ploy. "I agree. Let's distance ourselves from this despicable operation."

He permitted her to tug him away by the shoulder and continued on without glancing back around. Truth be told, she struggled not to break into hysteria, delighted by this fiery side of the mild-mannered man. She figured out what attracted him to her.

"I apologize for my rant," he expressed after they rounded a corner. "I can't tolerate people who exploit others."

"I don't like it, either." She didn't elaborate, still fighting the giggles.

They wandered toward the Ferris wheel, and he asked if she'd like to go on it. She agreed, despite her mother having always labeled them as dangerous. With the classic ride popular, the line stretched far back, making them wait for it to complete two rotations before their turn. A Black man and his young daughter stood in front of them, as the little girl fidgeted with excitement.

She put her head back, looking into the sky. "It's so tall, Daddy!"

Mabel stole a glimpse of Roy. He wore a wide smile, showing her what a good father he must've been. The child's elation tickled her, too.

Once the wheel finished its spin, guests exited off car-by-car, and the line started advancing again. The girl danced when her dad prodded her along to the front, where they waited for the ride's operator to grant them entry. The man handed the worker two tickets, but instead of accepting them and opening the gate, he ripped them up and threw them aside.

The white employee glared at him. "Don't bother giving me any more. I won't take them."

His gaze fell to the ground. "Don't worry. Those were my last two."

"What's wrong, Daddy? Can't we get on?"

"No, baby."

The worker untied a rope between the barriers beside them, motioning for them to leave. "Get off my station."

Before they exited, Roy tore off two tickets from his stash. "Perhaps you'll take them from me."

"Of course, sir, in a moment."

"No, you don't understand. These are for this gentleman and his beautiful daughter. If you don't take them, I'm afraid you can't have ours, either."

The man sneered. "What do I care? It doesn't matter how many of those pieces of garbage I collect. I have the right to deny access to my station to whoever I want, and now, I'm denying it to you."

"All right, I'll be sure to tell that to your boss." Roy remained mild, but his firm tone made his resolve clear.

To Mabel's surprise, the operator opened the gate to the man and girl, snatching the tickets out of Roy's hand. He didn't assist them into the seat the way she observed him do with the other parties, and he failed to do so for Mabel and Roy. Neither of them cared, as hearing the little one's cries of glee while they rode around made up for his hostility.

They ignored his insults when they exited afterward, and Roy took his kindness a step further. Hurrying up to the father and daughter, he ripped off another section of tickets and crouched down to give them to the girl. "You go on whatever you'd like."

She beamed, and Mabel could sense the father's gratification when he thanked Roy.

****

The two meandered along, not uttering a word about the confrontation. Mabel continued to marvel at the courage and kindness Roy displayed. Once again, she appreciated that she shouldn't underestimate this small-town factory worker.

They agreed to hop on the park's train, and she hoped he'd stick to the slower pace the whole night.

They made it to the platform right before it embarked on a new tour, boarding the half-full locomotive. Sitting a few rows from the back, they observed the property and neighboring Ohio River pass by in the dusky twilight. As she gazed out the window, she discerned his attention lingering on her, but she didn't peek over to confirm it in case it would spook him. The sensation alone elated her.

She admired the river's calm waves, with the sunset drawing out all its sparkles. Before long, her thoughts defied her resolution not to attach her current experiences to the past. The setting, along with Roy's gesture, conjured up that memory of her second night with Clark.

****

The Jennings family sat at a table in a park by Lake Michigan, finishing their supper. Mabel kept the picnic basket close by in an effort to conceal the food she secretly packed for Clark. After their run-in, she decided not to mention his plan to meet up with them. She reckoned if she wanted them to treat her like an adult, she shouldn't ask for permission the way a child would.

Clark couldn't leave the hotel until six, so she continued to check her watch and the parking lot. At a quarter after the hour, her anticipation grew, until her little sister popped it.

"Will you throw around the beach ball with me?"

She wanted to refuse, but she realized it would add more friction to the trip. She struggled to focus on the game, given her eyes kept shifting to the table she hoped Clark would spot. On one of her many sprints to retrieve the ball, she caught sight of him at last and held her breath as he approached her parents.

She made one more toss to her sister. "I'll be back."

The girl peered toward the table. "You sneak!"

She jogged from the sand to the grass, strapping on her sandals along her trek. When she skipped up to them, she listened to her mother's apology for neglecting to prepare him something. She lifted the basket, but Mabel raced to beat her to it.

She hustled to her side and grabbed it from her hands. "I can get that, Mom. I think I packed another sandwich in case we needed it."

Her mother's face showed her confusion at first, before a grin crossed her lips. "Now I understand why you offered to make up everything."

Her father let out a grunt, which she ignored, and she placed the food in front of Clark after he sat down. To her relief, he told her he loved ham on rye, and he cleaned it off his plate in short order. She handed him the peanuts, but before he began to munch on them, he nodded toward Millie.

"Your sister looks bored."

She followed his gaze to find Millie on the ground, rolling the ball between her outstretched legs. "Yeah, we were playing catch earlier."

"Why don't you go back to her? I'll head over once I'm done."

She shot a subtle glance in her dad's direction, uncertain she could trust him alone with her date. Instead of wearing the disapproving scowl she expected, his eyes displayed a hint of admiration, which she never detected in him around any other boy.

A few minutes later, Clark trotted down to the sand

and joined them. He took his position halfway between them, and Millie beamed in delight over his interest. He enhanced the excitement of the game by unexpectedly changing their rotation after a few rounds, even tossing the ball at one of them despite looking at the other. Before long, they took turns faking out one another, and even her parents played along after a while.

Mom and Dad tired out first. Millie groaned when they announced their desire to return to the hotel. Mabel didn't dare complain and endanger her father's warming attitude toward Clark.

"Can't we stay for fifteen more minutes?" Millie pleaded.

Mabel expected her dad to reaffirm his command, but to her astonishment, he shifted toward Clark. "Would it trouble you to drive them back?"

"Not at all, sir."

Millie leaped with glee and embraced their new friend.

****

With only one station, the engine stopped after a brief journey, snapping Mabel back to the present. After consulting her, Roy marched up to the engineer and forfeited another couple of tickets to secure them a second round. Others did the same, and since so few stood in wait for the next ride, they started chugging along again in short order.

Because nobody sat in close proximity to them, Mabel took advantage of their relative privacy. "I appreciated what you did for that young girl."

"Thank you, but I'm sad that doing the right thing makes you stand out. It should be commonplace. They deserve to enjoy life as much as we do."

She pondered his point, wishing again that she'd scrutinized society through better lenses. "We have these practices so ingrained in our culture here that the majority of us don't analyze our own thinking and actions. How has your community adapted?"

"We might be a tad ahead of you, but growing pains still plague us. I'm good friends with a Black man from work, and people stare at us wherever we go together. I joke that they're fascinated with my big nose. The criticism doesn't bother me. I've never met a better guy, and I pity others who can't open up their minds to that privilege."

His compassion touched her more still, but she chose not to offer another compliment in light of his profound statements. Instead, she strived to let his example seep down into her soul.

For the time being, the mood lightened when they exited the train and resumed their quest around the complex. Beyond his knowledge, Roy kept to her speed in terms of attractions, leading them to the paddle boats and a water show. She indulged him in joining him on the swing ride, which she preferred to avoid, but she opted out of the bumper cars and turnpike ride.

"Why would I want to drive a phony vehicle when I won't get behind the wheel of a real one?" she reasoned with him.

"Then why don't we try the roller coaster?" He gestured to the one in front of them.

She glared at the wooden structure. Despite her family's pleas and dares, none of them could ever persuade her to ride it since its construction in the early fifties. "I reckon I'll take a crack at driving. After all, the cars don't go more than three miles per hour, right?"

He gave her a sidelong glance, his lips creasing upward. "Hit a sore spot, did I?"

"Well, I think they've set a maximum age for coasters."

"Who told you that?" he asked.

Sweat began to form on her everywhere, but she remained nonchalant. "It's unspoken."

"So, how long ago did you last go on it?" He stayed kind in his demeanor, but she detected a challenging undercurrent in his tone.

"It didn't open until after I aged out."

"You've never ridden it, then?"

She crossed her arms. "Nope, and I've survived this long, if you can believe it."

"Don't tell me you haven't tried a roller coaster before."

"You mean a death trap that at least gives you a rush in your final moments? No, I haven't taken the opportunity."

"Ah, come on, Miss Jennings," he begged. "Here, I thought I was the square between the two of us."

"In all honesty, so did I." She enjoyed making the confession.

"If that's the case, you should take it from a square like me when I say you'll be fine."

"That's your pitch? I'll live through it?" she balked.

"You'll love it. Nothing invigorates you more than the rush of speeding through the air."

She took another gander at the ominous monstrosity, and beyond her control, a chuckle escaped her mouth. Roy interpreted that as consent, so he whisked her by the hand to the gate. She intended to use the minutes they spent in line to coerce him out of it, but with the crowd dwindling, they advanced to the front in time to get into the coaster for its next go-round. With no choice, she bent her legs and wiggled inside the tiny car, an even harder task for her tall date. When he wrapped his arm around her shoulder, she didn't take it too personally, given the small quarters didn't offer any other place.

Once they settled in as best they could, the contraption began its ascent up the menacing hill. Listening to the rollers underneath them click the whole way, Mabel assumed the sound matched the thudding of her heart. She wished she'd counted them so she could somehow dictate it to whoever made her tombstone. They passed the end of what she guessed to be a service ladder, which dashed her last hope of breaking free. Soon thereafter, the clicking stopped, relieving her, but the view ahead lent her no comfort.

She hoped to capture a mental photograph of the park in its entirety when they climbed to the peak, if for nothing more than to create one last memory. Before she seized the chance, the vehicle catapulted down, promising to drill them into the ground below. Right at the instant she expected to kiss her tush goodbye, the cars in front of theirs soared upward, lugging them along.

Everything faded into a blur after that, aside from the jerky way the machine jostled them. Mabel lost her sense of direction altogether, unable to recognize the terminal when they returned to it. As their speed started to decrease, pain in her hips and back set in from the erratic movements.

"Now, that didn't scare you too bad, did it?" Roy inquired.

"It gave me a thrill, all right."

He snickered, not pestering her for more positive feedback, and they waited for the ride to park at the exit. Afterward, she prepared to climb out, but Roy stayed put, preventing her from lifting a muscle.

"You aren't going to make me risk my life again, are you?" She didn't intend for her voice to sound so whiny.

He groaned. "No, I can't get out. That last bump did a number on my back."

She struggled not to break out into giggles while she gave him a supportive shove to assist him onto his feet. A young attendant hurried over to offer him a hand, and together, they succeeded. As they stepped away from it, she made sure his back didn't impair him from walking, but she couldn't face him, afraid of losing her composure.

"I guess there should be an age limit on those things."

His statement sent her straight into the hysterical fit she'd tried her best to contain. Through her squinted and tear-filled eyes, she noticed him crack a slight grin, until the humor of it overtook him, too. They laughed for most of their stroll to the front of the park.

With two tickets remaining in Roy's pocket, they decided to go on the carousel before they ventured out. Both being sore, they agreed to pass up the horses and take one of the carriages, instead. She always considered the ride romantic, and he enhanced it by grasping her hand for the first time.

They shared a comfortable silence for the first few

rotations, during which she contemplated the merry-go-round that sent her world spinning these past couple of days. Forty-eight hours earlier, Bev accused her of giving up on love, and in the short time that elapsed since, she realized she had. She didn't want to admit it to anyone, but she now realized how much it cost her to succumb to the fear of never finding someone to love her like Clark did.

Roy caught her gaze on him. "What's on your mind?"

She smiled and squeezed his hand. "I'm glad I took your call yesterday."

"So am I." He leaned down and planted a gentle kiss on her lips.

Chapter Four

After departing the park, Roy took her home, where they chatted in his truck at the curb for another twenty minutes. Exhaustion clouded his eyes while they visited, so Mabel told him they both needed to get some sleep. He offered to escort her to the door, but she refused, afraid he'd fall asleep on his ride to the hotel. Besides, it seemed ludicrous at her age to stand with a guy on her front steps and wait to find out if he would kiss her.

Even without following the tradition, Roy scooted closer to her and gave her a second smooch. Like the first, it wouldn't stir up a scandal, but it sent more shivers through her than any of her lip-locks with Ned. The smile he wore both times also added to her joy, reminding her of his confession at dinner the night before.

She marveled at how much she cared for him just a day after they met, but she experienced it in Chicago with Clark, too. Like she endured then, her heart hurt when she considered how little time they had left together. Though she soared out of bed the next morning, the realization soon struck her with force. This stranger who now meant so much to her would go home tomorrow, dropping out of her world in the whirlwind way he entered it.

She resolved not to dwell on the inevitable and

enjoy Roy's company while she could. She put on a cheery pink dress and endeavored to mask her inner gloom, but she couldn't fool Evelyn.

As she took a seat across from her at the breakfast table, the older woman regarded her with eyes of scrutiny. "The fried food from last night catching up with you?"

"No. Why?"

"You remind me of what I looked like when I took a bite of chop liver by accident. What's the matter? Not enough fireworks on your date?"

She shook her head. "I'm afraid there were too many."

Evelyn scoffed. "What's wrong with that? You can't tell me Mabel Jennings can't take the excitement anymore."

"No, I just can't take the letdown in the aftermath. The past couple of days have breathed life into me. I didn't realize I missed so much, but come tomorrow, it'll stop all at once."

"It doesn't have to. You can keep in touch and see where it goes. He asked for your number so he didn't have to rely on one of those flighty operators, if you recall."

She chuckled, appreciating how her friend could always perk up her outlook. With a better appetite, she munched on her toast, and the two discussed how Evelyn's garden fared amidst the dry start to summer. As she finished her meal, she noted the late hour and sped up her pace so she wouldn't miss her usual bus.

"I assume I'll have supper alone again?" Evelyn inquired while Mabel put on her shoes and hat.

Though she didn't sound sad, remorse struck

Mabel over leaving her for the past couple nights without much thought. She started to express her regret, before another epiphany occurred to her. "Roy didn't ask me out tonight, so I guess I'll stick around here. I can cook, since you've had to manage on your own."

"Oh, that doesn't bother me. I'll enjoy having you, but feel free to make plans with him if he gets ahold of you. He probably figures you have a standing invitation by now."

She grinned back at her on the way out the door. "Two days, and he's already taking me for granted like a wife."

Padding along, she pondered if Roy's failure to mention the next evening signaled anything. A part of her chided at the possibility Evelyn voiced, not liking the idea that he'd take such a casual approach at this point in their relationship. Still, her heart also sank when she considered he may have kept quiet because he didn't want to invite her out again.

Her contemplation slowed her pace enough that her bus took off right before she approached her stop. She bristled, aware she couldn't beat it to its next one, and she rushed to catch a different bus around the corner. The trip wouldn't be as direct as her regular route, but she had no other choice.

During the ride, she rationalized that if Roy decided to put a premature end to whatever they had going, she couldn't blame him. The brief moments they shared already made her dread their goodbye and prolonging it would only make it worse. He might've preferred to cap it off on a high note, and if so, she ought to appreciate his discernment.

Despite the delays, she arrived at the cord board

just a minute late. She apologized to Wendy for not relieving her on time and took the headset from her.

She shot her a teasing wink. "It's okay. Georgette clued me in on your big night with a handsome man."

"Speaking of which, a customer's requesting you." Georgette removed her headset and swapped it for the one in Mabel's hand.

Noting its plug stuck into the motel's jack, she didn't bother with formalities. "Good morning."

"Hi, there. Did I keep you up too late?" Roy asked.

With Wendy and Georgette both snooping, she gave her words careful consideration. "It was just one of those days. I didn't leave home as soon as I should've, and I missed my bus."

"Sounds like my son. He built up a month's worth of tardy marks during his freshman year of high school." The kindness in his voice kept her from taking offense at his comparing her to a kid. "Listen, honey, I forgot to tell you I have to go to dinner with some fellas from the factory tonight since tomorrow's my last day. I wondered if we could get together for lunch instead? I have a two-hour slot open in my schedule."

His statement evoked a variety of emotions in rapid succession. His term of endearment gave her pleasure she hadn't experienced in ages. Meanwhile, his reference to his upcoming departure reawakened her sadness. He made up for it with his invitation, which, she realized, elicited a response from her. "Sure, I can get away for an hour or so. What kind of place would you like?"

"I trust your judgement. That's worked out well for us so far."

"Well, don't get too confident until you get better

acquainted with me," she replied.

"I'm willing to take that challenge."

His comment and lack of hesitance when he made it warmed her cheeks along with her heart. "I'd better stay on this side of town so I can get back on time. Would you like me to give you directions to a place on Fourth Street and meet you?"

"Why don't you tell me how to get to your office and guide me from there? That way, you won't have trouble catching a bus."

She smiled and shook her head. "I'll ignore your hint of sarcasm and accept your kind gesture."

"Fair enough, Miss Jennings."

She advised him on the route to take and told him to wait for her in the lot behind the building. After their conversation concluded, Georgette began to josh her, but she stopped when their boss entered the room. His presence also prompted Wendy to vacate the area.

The morning proceeded with even more business than the past two, not permitting her to daydream about lunch. In fact, Georgette had to nudge her at five till twelve to remind her to take off for the elevator so she could beat the rush. Of course, she used the chance to bat her eyes in jest before Mabel could flee.

Once outside, she headed to the staff parking lot she visited on the few occasions Millie or Georgette gave her a lift. Roy's pickup stood out among the cluster of sedans, and it flattered her to discover him waiting for her beside it.

"I hope you haven't been standing out in this heat for too long."

He pecked her cheek before assisting her into the vehicle. "I haven't, but I'd consider it worthwhile if I had."

She helped him navigate to Oak to cut across to Fourth. She instructed him to park in front of a department store, and he shot her a puzzled glance as they entered it. She took advantage of his confusion, grasping his hand to lead the way.

When they approached the narrow stairwell, she let go of him and allowed him to follow her.

"I knew you didn't like me conning you into the roller coaster, but I didn't suppose it'd land me in a strange basement under a shopping market."

"Don't tell me the dark scares a tall, strong man like you," she joked.

"No, hitting my head on low ceilings daunts me more." His hunched posture attested to the fact.

It pleased her to make him squirm, getting her revenge for the previous day without intending to. A few steps down, the walls and ambiance lightened as the drab hallway spilled them into an airy restaurant. The wall in front of them featured a hand-painted mural of a country landscape, and its artist changed the tree in the foreground to fit each season. The bare, snow-covered branches she remembered from her last visit now popped with greenery, and marigolds circled the base of the trunk.

Teens lined the soda fountain counter, so Mabel and Roy took one of the tables.

"This is an impressive setup for such a quaint place," he said.

"Oh, this is for us nobodies, while the upper crust dines in the lavish place above the store. In all honesty, I don't envy them. The service is so slow. You can't get out of there in less than two hours. I can't fathom how people amass so much wealth when they squander the day away eating there."

He snickered. "Sounds like you're speaking from experience."

"My sister threw her engagement party there, and they've celebrated a couple of anniversaries there since. Her husband's family works in the coal industry, so I'm the pauper."

"It'd have to be a pretty magnificent kingdom for you to be the pauper in it." He winked and put his hand over hers.

A young woman arrived to take their drink orders. Again, they displayed similar tastes, both ordering milkshakes. Combing through her memory, she failed to drudge up even one instance when she and Ned made the same pick on any part of a meal. While she sipped on her strawberry shake and he on his chocolate one, he asked for her input regarding the menu's options. He took her suggestion of a BLT, but his eyes filled with trepidation upon noticing the green sauce on it when the waitress placed it on the table.

"Now I see the big picture. The nice décor distracts you from recognizing you're being poisoned."

She put on an offended expression. "Mr. Stentz, you've accused me of leading you into danger and having you poisoned all within the course of fifteen minutes. I can't imagine why you invited me out to eat."

"I guess I'm a risk-taker." He shrugged. "Tell me the truth, though. What kind of spread is this?"

"Their homemade mayo and the best part of the sandwich. Trust me...if you dare to." She gave him a maniacal grin.

He bit into it and began to nod after a moment of consideration. "I apologize for questioning your tastes."

"I accept that. For your information, it only made me sick once." When he leveled an alarmed frown at her like she desired, she cackled.

They both quieted down for the rest of the meal, with their allotted time ebbing away from them. The minutes raced away too fast in her opinion, following suit with the week thus far. While she finished her coleslaw, she began to wonder if they'd meet again after this, given his work commitments that evening. He told her the prior night he planned to start his journey home once he wrapped up at the factory Thursday, so she doubted another opportunity would arise.

As usual, he seemed to read her thoughts. "Since we can't squeeze in dessert now, do you think I could swing by after my dinner to have one with you and Evelyn?"

She decided to test him. "Oh, I assumed the shakes were dessert."

"Not to me." He aced it.

Given she'd already eaten more sweets around him than she did with any other man, she pretended to think it over for good measure. "I'm sure Evelyn would enjoy it. We'll make you something. Do you have a request?"

"I love peanut butter, but I'm not picky. I haven't baked many treats the past few years, so I doubt you can disappoint me."

She smirked, leaning in closer. "I won't bother trying, then."

He glanced at his watch and called for the waitress to retrieve the check for him. Upon putting down the tip, he extended his hand to Mabel and escorted her upstairs and out the door. Though their ride back to the phone company didn't take long, he managed to make it interesting.

"Have you ever considered learning to drive?" he asked.

"Sure, like I've considered my funeral plans. In fact, I find the two accompany each other."

"Boy, you seem to think about death an awful lot."

"Well, pardon me, but I'd like to live to see it," she quipped.

****

Mabel managed to get through the rest of the afternoon with only a few questions from Georgette, with both of them too busy to chat. She ended her day fifteen minutes later than usual to compensate for her late entrance and extended lunch. Nonetheless, she called Evelyn to inform her of Roy's plan to drop over, and they struck the deal that Evelyn would cook their meal while Mabel prepared dessert. She didn't mention the need to dust and tidy up the kitchen, but she added it to her own to-dos.

Hence, her departure mirrored her hurried arrival, with her running to the grocery store on the way home. She cringed when Roy mentioned peanut butter being his favorite, given she finished off their last jar that morning. Because of his kindness and generosity, along with his charm, she wanted to give him something special, despite it costing her an extra errand.

She hadn't made many peanut butter desserts and couldn't think of anything besides cookies. Evelyn refrained her, since she didn't enjoy them much, least of all peanut butter ones. Mabel often joked that her dislike of cookies could have crumbled their friendship and living arrangements. In an effort to satisfy them all, she opted to make a multi-layered bar, grabbing flour, oatmeal, and chocolate with a concept in mind. She didn't take great pride in her baking skills, never one to deviate from her typical recipes. With those ingredients, however, she figured she couldn't go wrong.

The fleeting time proved to be her biggest hurdle, and she spent most of her and Evelyn's meatloaf dinner on her feet. Consulting Evelyn on the dish she planned, she melted the chocolate to put a layer of it over the oatmeal base. After sticking it in the refrigerator for a while, she added a coating of peanut butter to the top. In between steps, she cleaned the entire first story, needing to change her clothes once she finished because of how much she'd sweat.

As she returned the bottle of furniture polish to the cleaning closest, the doorbell rang. She smoothed her skirt before gripping the doorknob. She noticed Roy's suit, the same one he wore to lunch, lost its crispness, and he'd taken off his tie.

He appeared tired, but she welcomed the introduction to this casual side of him. "Long time, stranger."

Roy put a hand on her left cheek while kissing the right one. "Almost too long."

She led him into the kitchen, where Evelyn sat, waiting. After the two greeted each other, Evelyn gave him a flirty smile. "You set me up to get a new dessert and see a handsome man. I like the way you think."

He raised his finger to his lips and replied in a whispering tone, "Don't let on to her that we hatched this scheme together."

Mabel feigned shock, laying spoons on the table

and then serving the two. "How'd your dinner go?"

"I didn't enjoy it as much as my last couple, but I managed. I've learned quite a bit from the guys here."

"Will you buy the machines you examined for your company?" Still at a loss on the particulars, she hoped her vagueness didn't give away her lack of comprehension.

"My bosses have to make the final decision, but I'm sure going to persuade them."

"From the little I've heard about you, I have a feeling you'll win them over." Evelyn winked at him. "Do you have any idea how long we've been pushing this one to go on a date and a roller coaster, for that matter? You talked her into both within two days of meeting her."

Mabel's cheeks heated up, so she took her first bite of her creation in an attempt to conceal her blushing. She savored the treat more than she anticipated and won high praise from her taste-testers. The combination of the three flavors made for a delicious blend, as did the contrast of the different textures. In an odd way, it symbolized her bond with Roy. She wouldn't have predicted their different backgrounds and personalities to mix very well, but when they fused together on their own, they formed a surprising delight.

When they finished, Evelyn insisted on washing the dishes and encouraged them to go for a walk. Mabel complied, and instead of strolling down the road, she suggested they drive to the nearby park. She considered it one of the most picturesque sites in the city, but due to her busy schedule and Evelyn's diminished mobility, she couldn't go often. Upon arriving, they followed the path that offered the best views of the property. Roy put his arm around her shoulder while they ventured along, admiring the rolling hills and vistas surrounding Beargrass Creek.

After wandering for a few minutes in silence, Roy struck up a conversation. "You and Evelyn seem to work well together. Living arrangements like yours don't suit everybody."

"We have our moments of getting tired of each other, but we've developed a good routine over the years. She's the best friend I've ever had, to tell you the truth. At first, I intended to stay just for however long it took me to get back up on my feet, but I couldn't leave. I observe her get frailer by the day and dread losing her."

His face took on a somber cast. "I struggled with the same angst during my wife's illness. Her doctor told us she wouldn't live six months after her diagnosis, but my strong girl made it past a year. I forced my heart to block out anything but gratitude for every hour with her. No matter how hard I tried, though, my mind always panned to the reality ahead, especially with each sign of her worsening condition."

She stroked his hand. "I'm sorry. I've experienced losing someone slowly and also suddenly, and I can't say I prefer one to the other. They're both painful."

"Your husband suffered a brain aneurism, you said?"

She nodded. "We didn't have any warning. He worked with a landscaping crew in town, and he collapsed as he trimmed some hedges. I relived that morning countless times in my head to pinpoint something I missed, but I never could."

He lured her close and kissed her cheek, before he

tensed. "I'm sorry for the crack I made this afternoon about you thinking of death too much. I forgot you have reason to."

He didn't grasp the truth in his words, but she didn't want to spoil their time together by revealing it to him. "Don't worry. My family would tell you I was born a coward."

"You aren't when it matters." He grinned and gave her another quick peck. The gesture reassured her he didn't disapprove of her divorce, even without the details.

Having only an hour left of sunlight, they couldn't traverse the whole trail, but she made sure they reached the stretch of forest known as Lovers' Lane before nightfall. She used to hope her dates would lead her to the secluded area. Boys took their girlfriends there to pin them and claim them forever...which usually lasted a month, tops. To her disappointment, none of her beaus did.

Of course, she didn't expect Roy to pin her and shared neither the area's name nor its reputation with him. Even so, it seemed to enhance his romantic side, as he leaned against the fountain right outside the wooded path and wrapped his arms around her middle. He kissed the back of her neck as they admired the sunset.

Several cars passed by them on the loop's lane for motorists, which must've reminded him of their brief discussion in the truck. To her disappointment, it crowded out his lustful demeanor and yielded to a notion she didn't appreciate.

"What makes you so opposed to driving?"

Her relaxed body stiffened. "I'm not. I just have

chosen not to. You recall how uncommon it used to be for women to get a license."

"I thought you said it had nothing to do with your being a woman."

Of all times for a man to listen to her. "That's correct, and like I also told you, I don't trust cars."

"One day, you may not have a choice, considering how buses are starting to disappear," he told her.

"Are they? Man, if I have a hard time catching one now, what am I going to do when they're invisible?"

"My point exactly." He chuckled. "Would you let me give you a quick lesson once we reach the truck? This would be the ideal place for it."

Sweat formed on her palms. "I appreciate your thoughts, but I don't want to. I doubt I could pick up much in such a short period, and I'm tired. I don't foresee Louisville getting rid of bussing anytime soon."

"Maybe not, but it'd save you a whole lot of hassle. Give me a chance."

Like the previous day, she obliged him, letting him usher her to the parking lot. He sped up his pace, his enthusiasm clear, and she teetered between being tickled and irritated by it. Although his concern complimented her, she bristled at him forcing her into something, especially a well-founded fear. Plus she hated for him to hasten their beautiful stroll.

When he handed her the keys, she protested some more, but he wouldn't relent. He maneuvered her into the driver's seat and closed her inside. The air became heavy, and she couldn't keep her fingers from trembling. She could only think about the tragedy after the beach picnic.

****

After their parents left the beach, Mabel, Clark, and Millie resumed their game, before taking a walk beside the water. As the sun crested on the lake, Mabel and Clark allowed Millie to go ahead of them, which gave them privacy to link hands. She no longer noticed the chilly spray trickling on her ankles, with all her attention drawn to the warmth of his touch.

Once darkness set in, they retreated to Clark's car. When they made it to the street that led to the hotel, a long line of traffic halted their journey. With no other route to take, they had to wait it out. They crawled their way foot by foot, with Mabel growing ever more worried about upsetting her parents.

With a block to go, they encountered police cars and an ambulance surrounding the crashed vehicles that caused the backup. The darkness prevented them from seeing details, but Mabel could make out the outline of a semitrailer. Lying in the ditch, it appeared to have swerved into the opposing lane and collided with a car. Clark followed the officer's instruction to veer around the scene, and though her conscience beckoned her not to, Mabel fixed her sights on the other car.

From the shape of it, she guessed it to be a sedan, but with its front end smashed, she couldn't identify its make. A lamppost stood a few yards away, helping her detect its green cast beneath all the damage. She swallowed hard but forced away the panic, keeping in mind that many vehicles shared the color.

But then Clark's headlights illuminated the Kentucky license plate.

****

Petrified by the experience to this day, she wiped

the beads of sweat off her forehead. She persisted in her argument the instant Roy hopped into the cab. "I can't do this, Roy."

"Nonsense. I taught my son the basics in less than fifteen minutes."

Surrendering, she placed the key in the ignition but struggled to get it to fit into the spot. Roy grabbed it and spun it over with a grin. She wanted to use her gaffe to aid her argument, but her mouth remained closed during his instructions about the clutch and gear shift. The process always daunted her, but his calm, amiable manner helped her absorb it. When the moment arrived for her to step on the clutch, a hint of exhilaration triumphed over her terror.

She shifted into first gear and eased her foot from the brake onto the gas pedal. The truck inched its way forward but stalled an instant later. Roy commanded her to slowly lift her foot off the clutch. She restarted it and tried again with success, and to her bafflement, they advanced forward under her control. She couldn't repress a giggle as she circled the lot, which didn't hold any other vehicles in it. Roy gave her permission to accelerate after she finished a lap, so with newfound confidence, she applied more pressure to the gas.

Once the speedometer passed the ten mile per hour mark, the engine made a rumbling noise, alarming her, but he reminded her of the need to shift gears. She replayed his lecture in her mind, but another car approached them and interrupted her thought pattern. Her memory of her ruined family car flooded back to her.

She cranked the wheel to the right to avert any chance of a collision. To her dismay, her paranoia blinded her from the tree straight ahead of her, and she slammed into it.

"What happened?" Roy exclaimed.

"I listened to a man I hardly know, that's what happened!" She opened the door with fervor. "I vowed never to compromise who I am for someone again, and look at me. I gave you the wrong impression, Mr. Stentz, and I apologize for that. When you go home tomorrow, I hope you'll do me the favor of forgetting about me, and I'll try to do the same."

She stalked toward the exit, ignoring his pleas to stop.

Chapter Five

Mabel remained by the payphone booth like she told Millie she would, peering at the park from across the street. She'd stormed out through a different gate than the one she and Roy entered, in hopes he wouldn't find her as he exited. He could loop around to locate her if he wanted to, but after ten minutes passed without her spotting him, she figured he didn't bother.

Before long, she caught sight of the pearl white convertible Millie's husband, Daryl, surprised her with for their tenth anniversary. Mabel always shook her head at the notion of a family needing—and being able to afford—two vehicles.

Opening the door of the showpiece, she didn't have both legs inside when her sister began to bandy.

"Let me guess: He didn't pin you on Lovers' Lane."

Mabel crossed her arms. "Nope, he can't commit to you unless you're a licensed driver."

Millie's jaw dropped. "Is that true?"

"I don't know, and I couldn't care less. He may have wanted to teach me so he could go home with a puffed chest and tell all those northerners how he rescued a hillbilly from public transportation."

"You drove? Boy, I would've paid money to witness that."

"That's another indicator of too much wealth." She

never hesitated to voice her disapproval of their luxurious lifestyle. "Although I must admit the spectacle wouldn't have set you back a great deal. It didn't last long and ended with a bang."

Millie gave her a stern grimace. "Don't tell me you wrecked his car. Mabel, we need to go back and give him a ride."

"I didn't leave more than a nick on the bumper, but I flipped my lid. It just reminded me of…"

Millie set her hand over her sister's and completed her sentence in a whisper, "Daddy."

She nodded but let out a sniff to force away the emotion. "For whatever it's worth, I did more damage to Ned's truck when he gave me a lesson. I backed into the barn and ruined the latch on the bed. On the bright side, he didn't pressure me to drive again."

"Did you tell Roy what happened to Mom and Dad?"

"No, I already told him how Clark died, and I didn't want to give him the impression I'm a calamity crier. Besides, I never told Ned the whole story, either. I almost did a couple of times, but it didn't seem right. I suppose my heart read his character sooner than my brain did."

Millie raised a brow at her. "You aren't saying Roy's another Ned, are you? If that's the case, I can't believe you'd go out with him three nights in a row."

"Not at all. He's genuine, kind, and accepting. He didn't blink when Evelyn mentioned my divorce, and you should've seen the way he spoke to a little Black girl at Fountaine Ferry. That's why it shocked me when he acted so insistent tonight."

"I understand, but it sounds to me like he wouldn't

have if you would've explained it to him. He seems to have merited your trust."

"How can you determine that after two days?"

She shrugged. "It didn't take you longer than that with Clark."

A faint smile flashed across her lips. She appreciated her sister's point, aware this whole time she was reliving her youth in spite of her own resolve not to. "Ned taught me not to expect anyone to measure up to Clark, even if I spot some similarities. Remember how I swooned when he gave me a rose at the wedding where we met? It didn't take me long to figure out he just couldn't resist a freebie."

Millie shook her head. "But all the same, you can't give up on every single man because of Ned Banks. You can't give up on yourself, either. You may have made a mistake by falling for him like that, but as you said, you learned from it."

Mabel sighed and shifted toward the window. "Maybe. Clark and I faced so many challenges, but accepting each other for who we were didn't pose any problem. He never tried to change me, and I didn't him. Ned, on the contrary, couldn't find anything about me he didn't have to fix. I often wanted to ask him why he married me in the first place. Roy's kind, but I'm afraid he'll do the same thing. He leveraged me into riding a roller coaster and—"

She broke out laughing. "Stop right there. He persuaded you to ride a roller coaster? My sister, the hypochondriac who's scared any kind of adrenaline rush will send her to the emergency room?"

Mabel grinded her teeth. "Now I understand why my niece thinks I'm a bore. She gets it from you."

"No, sis, you've convinced her of that all on your own."

Mabel zipped her lips, tired of defending her concept of fun. During the remainder of the drive, she reflected on her hasty exit. Roy may have come on stronger than she preferred, but he didn't compare to Ned's harshness. She agreed with Millie's assessment of him and wished she'd revealed the cause for her anxiety.

Out of the corner of her eye, she observed her sister, and her mind wandered back to that night.

****

Officers who'd already identified their parents awaited the girls in the hotel lobby and drove them to the hospital. To Mabel's surprise, Clark followed behind them. When they arrived at the emergency room, the desk clerk informed them both their parents remained in surgery. She explained their mom suffered significant injuries to her pelvis, but the doctors attending to her gave priority to her lung damage. The girls couldn't get much information about Dad, but the clerk assured them one of his physicians would meet with them whenever they had something to report.

They sat down in the waiting area. Clark stayed near the entrance, appearing uncertain of whether he'd overstep if he drew closer. With Millie's head on her shoulder, Mabel motioned for him to take the seat beside her. He obliged her and encircled her hand with both of his. They froze in place for an endless period in Mabel's estimation, until a doctor approached them.

"Mabel Jennings?"

She stood. "Yes, sir."

"According to my colleagues, your mother's

recovering from surgery, and you may see her in her room after a while. I helped treat your dad and am afraid he didn't fare as well."

Millie strode to her sister's side. "What do you mean?"

He lowered his eyes but faced them straight on to share the news. "We lost him."

****

She dabbed away a tear and tried not to dwell on the rest. When they made it to her and Evelyn's house, she thanked Millie for the lift but scurried out of the car before her sister could lecture her some more. Once inside, she let out a sigh of relief upon discovering Evelyn already retreated to bed. She couldn't face hearing her input right away. Not inclined to do much of anything, she padded straight to her bedroom, wondering whether or not she'd ever see Roy Stentz again.

****

Descending the stairs, Mabel prepared to execute her mission of telling Evelyn as little as possible about her spat with Roy. Overnight, she appreciated the advantages of making a somewhat clean break, with him leaving today and all. They'd both return to their separate lives, and he'd have a comical anecdote to take back to his small town. She remembered how much the locals in Irvington ate up something like that.

She entered the kitchen and caught Evelyn skipping her usual bowl of oatmeal to indulge in one of the bar cookies.

"I see you're getting off to a healthy start today."

"Why not? You put oatmeal in here, didn't you? It has eggs and protein, too. I finished off the dish so you

85

can make another one." She gestured toward the empty container by the sink.

She shook her head, albeit rather amused. "We only ate a third of this at supper. No wonder you fell asleep so early."

"You should take it as a compliment, my dear." She patted her hand as Mabel sat down with a bowl of cereal. "I tried my best to stay up to hear about your walk, but I couldn't. Tell me, did you two go down Lovers' Lane?"

"We took that part of the path, but he didn't notice the sign. He enjoyed the scenery."

"Particularly the pretty lady on his arm, no doubt." She gave her a wink.

Mabel kept her eyes on her breakfast, hating to deceive her. "It capped off his trip nicely. I'm glad you suggested it."

"Anything I can do to further romance, even if it isn't mine."

Her beaming face sent guilt through Mabel, and she lost her appetite to eat the rest of her meal. Dumping it into the trash, she justified it by saying she poured too much. Her watch told her she didn't need to leave for half an hour, but she couldn't bear to stick around and lie. For once, she preferred to deal with the girls at work as opposed to Evelyn.

Right before she told her she wanted to get a head start, the doorbell rang. She counseled her friend to stay put, and she headed into the foyer. When she opened the door, Roy stood on the doorstep with a contrite grin.

"Morning, Miss Jennings."

"Hello, Mr. Stentz. I trust your truck still runs all right?"

Her statement seemed to perplex him at first, but it dawned on him after a moment. "Oh, yes, you didn't damage anything."

"That's good to hear. You won't have trouble making it home."

"No, but I've decided not to take off until tomorrow. I'd like to make up for last night. I realize I overstepped my place, and I'm so sorry I gave you the idea I wanted to change you. I understand why you accused me of it, but believe me when I say I adore you for who you are. I owe you my sincerest apology, as well as a nice dinner, if you'll let me."

She debated the invitation, conflicted. Although she didn't want him to return home with them on bad terms, delaying the inevitable would only hurt both of them more. She reckoned if she kept her expectations in check, she could oblige him. If nothing else, he could leave with a clean conscience. On the same line, an idea occurred to her that would serve to cleanse her own.

"I'll go along with that if you wouldn't mind driving me to work. I'd like to show you something else in the neighborhood."

He agreed to her deal, appearing relieved, and she darted inside to grab her purse and tell Evelyn she was leaving early. Of course, the older woman surmised Roy's presence, and her face lit up with glee. Tickles of excitement fluttered through Mabel, but dread over her plan accompanied them. Even so, she didn't want to regret not doing this in retrospect.

Per her instruction, he continued straight for a couple of miles before he took a left. Despite her closeness to it, she made few treks to Ewing, with it inflicting too much pain for her to handle. So intense, she even struggled to accept Evelyn's initial offer for her to live there.

As always, the ride down the road took her back to the day she traveled it with Clark.

****

Passing the welcome sign when they entered the city limits, the sense of belonging didn't surge through Mabel like it did at the end of most road trips. In fact, no emotion at all blanketed her broken heart. Judging by the silence in the car, she gathered her mom and sister struggled with the same. For the past week, they trudged along in a state of numbness, and she wondered if they'd ever emerge from the empty vessels that had enveloped them. Assuming they would break out of this hollow trance, she dreaded the pain that may well drown them.

She couldn't even enjoy the extra hours with Clark as he drove them home. Instead, she wallowed in despair over the way their time together ended. He'd stuck by her side every day and tended to their needs however he could. Her affectation for him grew by the hour, but so did her realization that they couldn't continue their romance. With the responsibilities now thrust upon her, she couldn't devote the attention he deserved.

Parking in front of their house on Ewing Street, Clark climbed out of the car to help her mom, who could now walk but with a limp. Mabel and Millie unloaded the luggage. They only stopped once during the six-hour journey, so her stiff muscles protested the heavy lifting. Her father had scolded the three of them for packing too much, but it worked out well given their need to extend their trip.

After he settled her mom into her chair, Clark met them at the door to carry a few of their bags upstairs as they directed. For the time being, Mabel couldn't peek inside for longer than an instant without her dad's blatant absence crippling her with grief. Once she handed Clark the last of the suitcases, she sat down on the front steps. She trained her gaze in the opposite direction of her loss, but she couldn't escape it.

A few minutes later, Clark asked if he could join her, and she agreed. She put her hand in his and leaned her head against his shoulder, neither uttering a word. They barely spoke after they learned of the crash, but the lack of communication did nothing to weaken their bond.

As the sunlight vanished, their moments together waned with it.

"Are you sure you can't stay the night here?" she asked him. "I can go to my apartment so you can sleep in my room. I don't want you to fall asleep on the road."

"I wish I could, but since I have to go right back to work the day after tomorrow, I need to head north. I promise I'll stop in Indianapolis." He wrapped his arm around her, already acquainted with her new fear of accidents. "You really think you can handle this on your own?"

Her instinct beckoned her to tell him she couldn't, but it wouldn't do anything besides add to their shared misery. "We'll be okay. Millie can help out a lot, especially after she finishes school. She gets on my nerves, but every time I see her now, a measure of peace washes over me."

He kissed her forehead. "I'm glad you have each

other."

"Thank you so much for everything. I can't fathom
how I would've endured this without you." She yearned
to say more, but she couldn't conjure up a way to
express her true feelings. Thus she huddled close to him
in silence, struggling to comprehend how love and
heartbreak could coexist like they did inside her.

When he stood, his eyes told her similar emotions
tore through him. He mustered a single request. "Write
to me, please? I'll do the same."

She hesitated, before she nodded despite her tears.

****

She sighed, refusing to cry, and focused on her
goal. The short street welcomed two new houses since
she left it, but the landscape remained unchanged
otherwise. The one difference made her avoid the area,
and her stomach rolled with unsettled anxiety the
instant they approached it. She commanded Roy to stop
and to park in front of it. The boarded-up windows and
dilapidated exterior of the once beautiful white cottage
never ceased to horrify her. She averted her gaze from
the porch where Clark held her.

"I grew up here. My dad's parents gave it to him
and my mom because they couldn't maintain it
anymore. I loved everything about this house, from the
smell of its cedar floors to the bay window in the sitting
room. It provided such a spectacular view of the
sunrise.

"Dad worked for the better part of twenty years to
pay off the mortgage they put on it after Mom had my
sister. They managed to hold onto their home through
the Depression when most of the neighbors couldn't.
But before they paid the loan in full, he died in a car

accident during our trip to Chicago. Someone veered into his lane and hit him head-on."

"Oh, my," Roy muttered.

"My mom rode with him that night, and her injuries crippled her for life. She insisted Millie finish school like I had, so I moved back home to support the three of us. I planned to do everything in my power to help Mom stay here, and we made it all right for the first year. I married my husband the next spring, and he earned enough to feed us and pay the bills. After we lost him, we couldn't swing it, so we ended up in government housing."

He stroked her hand. "Sounds like you did the best you could, honey."

She acknowledged it and swallowed hard, still finding it difficult to accept the situation. She neglected to tell him about the countless times she wondered what would've happened if they would've ridden to the hotel together that night. Would it have changed anything for the better, or would they all have suffered injury?

She resisted diving into the bottomless pool of *what ifs* and focused on making her point. "I'd toyed with the idea of driving prior to that, but afterward, I couldn't face the prospect. On the few occasions I've given it a try, including last night, my mind goes to that day and everything it cost us."

"That's understandable. I wish I'd known." His deep voice had a softness to it she'd never heard in anybody before.

"I'm sorry I didn't explain it last night. I hated to ruin our final evening, and I haven't shared it for a long time. Plus my first husband helped me through a lot of it. We met and fell in love on that very trip, and he stepped in to support us in whatever way he could. He stayed up all night to sit with us at the hospital after the crash and even took two days off of work to drive us home. I guess I like to keep that story just for us."

He nodded his head. "I go through the same when it comes to my wife. Some pried for the details of her symptoms and diagnosis, but I can't summon the strength to reveal more than necessary. I want to preserve the time we spent together, rather than share it with others who are just nosey."

She grasped his hand and laced her fingers around his. "I understand."

"You're so full of life; no one could fathom the tragedy you've endured."

"I struggled for a long time, but being so young when it happened made me realize I didn't want to spend decades in misery. Misery compounds on itself until it's too high a mountain to climb off."

"I can attest to that," he murmured.

They fell into a moment of silence, each clearly mourning their losses. Since she'd begun the sad reflection, she took the initiative to draw it to a close. "I didn't mean to put a damper on your day."

"You didn't. You just reminded me why I'm not in a hurry to leave you." He leaned over and gave her a kiss.

****

On the rest of the ride, Mabel showed Roy various landmarks from her childhood, such as where her schoolhouse used to stand and the event complex that hosted the annual circus. The commute flew by faster than usual, both because of the lack of stops and the amiable atmosphere. She couldn't have imagined them on such good terms less than an hour earlier.

Before he left her off at the building, he piqued her curiosity by telling her he already chose where he wanted to take her for dinner and didn't need directions how to get there. Adding to her wonderment, he advised her to dress on the formal side. She later assumed he must be taking her to wherever he dined the previous evening. Just the same, she resolved not to take anything for granted with this kind-hearted man.

Waiting for the elevator, she pondered what the night may hold in store, but Lorna's arrival cut her daydreaming short. Like she'd expect, the bride-to-be glowed with joy.

She looped arms with Mabel. "So, the whispers are true?"

You mean the whispers that say you're hearing voices? "Pardon me?"

"Rumor's spreading that you're seeing a new beau. Since you haven't mentioned it to me, I didn't believe it until I spotted that fellow drop you off. Why wouldn't you let me in on the secret?"

Because I don't like you, that's why. "I didn't want to take away from your big day this weekend."

"Nonsense! When love is in the air, sharing it makes it even better. I couldn't be jealous of you. At your age, it's such a marvelous surprise."

"The eighth world wonder," Mabel muttered.

The doors opened and allowed her to shuffle away from the girl, but with nobody else inside the elevator, she couldn't shed Lorna's rapt attention.

"So, what's his name?"

"Roy. He's here on business from Pennsylvania."

"Really? I didn't think Yankees drove pickups."

"He lives in the country. They come in handy in rural communities." She remembered the fact well.

Though Lorna introduced the subject of his vehicle in the first place, she hastened to dismiss it. "Listen, Rodney and I have a couple of extra place settings left over from guests who can't attend the wedding. You two are still welcome."

Mabel could sort out her real motives—a gift and some juicy gossip to tell after she ran out of stories from her honeymoon. "I wish we could, but he's going home tomorrow."

Unlike Monday, she manifested genuine disappointment. "Oh, I'm sorry to hear that. Well, as I said before, you can change your RSVP if your schedule changes. I'm not working tomorrow, so you'll have to give me a call."

She offered the empty assurance that she would and congratulated her, hoping she wouldn't have to again. In the seven months following her engagement, Lorna coerced the word out of her almost every week. Once the elevator spilled them out on the phone company's floor, Mabel darted off for the restroom so she wouldn't have to follow her any longer.

The board didn't brim with activity through the morning like it did at the beginning of the week. She predicted traffic would pick up in the afternoon when people started making weekend plans. During her lunch break, she realized, for the first time all week, she hadn't received a call from Roy. Given he drove her to work, she understood, but she'd be lying if she claimed it didn't sow an emptiness inside her. Bothering her more, she wouldn't get another chance after today.

She cast the thought away, choosing to concentrate

on their supposedly fancy date. In between conversations with customers, she contemplated her wardrobe options. She didn't attend many formal events in recent years, so she hadn't bought a gown in ages. At her sister's parties, she opted to wear what she already owned because of her lack of excitement for such elaborate affairs.

She couldn't help but wish she'd splurged and debated shopping for something suitable on her way home. Fearing it would make her late, she repressed the urge and resigned to make do with whatever she could unearth from the back of her closet. At the same time, she strived not to let her expectations soar too high. His definition of formal may differ from hers. After all, he wore two suits during his stay, and she wouldn't term either of them elegant.

Sorting through her clothes, she began to lose heart as she examined her standard attire. Right before she yielded to her frustration and canceled with Roy, a silk, magenta evening dress sparkled in the shadows. She stretched out to take hold of its hanger, still adoring it despite its marred history. She bought it when she was married to Ned and under his meager clothing allowance, and he didn't take it well when she paid five dollars more than he allotted her. She smiled, pleased to get to wear it for somebody who'd value the way she looked instead of what it cost.

Considering her lenience with her diet after the divorce, she questioned how it would fit, and it filled her with glee when she zipped it up with no trouble. A matching scarf accompanied it, which made it worth the extra money in her estimation. She tossed both ends over her shoulder. Paired with the frock's draped neckline and lack of sleeves, it created a dramatic ensemble unlike anything she'd worn since her youth.

Her favorite ivory fascinator complemented it, too. To complete the look, she sorted through her lipstick shades and chose an almost exact match to the color of the dress. She gave her reflection a final once-over, delighted, and grabbed a shawl in case of an evening breeze.

Waiting in the living room, Evelyn applauded when Mabel modeled it. "My, my! Didn't you tell me half an hour ago you wouldn't overdo it because the country guy might deem a hoedown a formal occasion?"

"Well, he asked for it. The joke's on him if everyone else arrives in jeans and flannel."

"I'd say. Where did you have that beauty hidden away?"

"The dungeon part of my wardrobe. I forgot about it after all these years. I purchased it for a wedding Ned and I would've attended if I hadn't left him the month before. The miser blew a fuse over the price, but seeing as it was his cousin getting married, I refused to return it."

Evelyn winked. "His loss and Roy's gain."

A knock echoed from the door, and she rushed to open it. Roy awaited her in a white dinner jacket. His French cuffs extended underneath its sleeves, and as he crossed the threshold, she noted the black bowtie around his collar. *Roy Stentz dressed up for her*, she thought with satisfaction.

He greeted her with a peck on the cheek and regarded her from head to toe. The adoration in his eyes emitted the message she'd longed to receive ever since she lost Clark.

"You're ravishing."

She thanked him, self-conscious all of a sudden. As always, she covered it with humor. "You clean up well, too. I didn't anticipate you'd brought something so dapper."

"To be honest, I didn't. I used my afternoon off to do some shopping. I can't recall the last time I bought a new suit."

She winked. "I'm honored."

Ever the gentleman, he strolled across the room to address Evelyn. "Where's your gown?"

She chuckled at his joke and returned one of her own. "I lent it to her. I'll have it ready to go for tomorrow if you're interested."

The trio laughed, before Evelyn wished them a good time. Roy encircled his arm through Mabel's as he escorted her outside, making her giddy like a girl going to the spring formal with the school's most popular guy. She struggled a little more than normal to hop into his truck because of the snug fit of the tea-length dress. Her efforts to avert an embarrassing incident served to distract her from her sorrow over their last journey together.

Her lack of knowledge of their destination also preoccupied her, making her calculate the possibilities with each street he took. Within two blocks, she determined they were headed back downtown, which did nothing to narrow down the potential venues. When he trekked onto Fourth and parked in the same spot he did the day before, she caught on to his scheme.

Not wanting to seem presumptuous, she played coy. "So, you liked the scary basement this much, huh?"

"I did, but that isn't where we're going. Your stellar review of the place upstairs made me want to experience it."

"Remind me of the stellar part. Was it my reference to the snobby patrons or the slow service?"

He snickered. "Both, as a matter of fact. For one, I want to prove what a pauper you're not, which you've already done all on your own. And two, I'm happy to milk this evening out for as long as possible."

She wondered if charisma came naturally or if he'd learned it from somebody, but either way, he perfected it. Shimmying onto the sidewalk, she opened her handbag to take out her gloves, a must in the glamorous banquet hall. Glad she carried a decent pair, she slipped them on before she took his hand and pointed to the elevator once inside the building. They took it to the sixth floor and weaved their way through the store's china department, careful not to get too close to the breakables.

Not having gone in several years, she couldn't figure if they redecorated the restaurant or if her memory failed her. The room's yellow walls shined brighter, and the gold light fixtures glistened with even more shimmer than she recalled. Upon further inspection, she recognized most of its other features and discerned the decor hadn't changed, but her perception of it did. At Millie's celebrations, she served as no more than a guest who smiled for photos and presented the most modest gift on the table. Roy, on the contrary, counted her special enough to invite her here to enjoy her company and give them both a memory to cherish later.

Without delay, the door attendant led them to a table by the large windows overlooking the city. The waitresses lived up to their reputation for slowness, but remembering Roy's line of reasoning, Mabel didn't fret over it. Rather, she used the time to peer around with her newfound appreciation for the place. She gazed at the orchids painted on the walls' borders and marveled at the intricacy of each one. She wondered if the same artist responsible for the mural downstairs painted them, too. The dazzling chandeliers hanging above them also captivated her interest. Even the yellow leather chairs, which complemented the walls, seemed more comfortable when she sat across from him.

Roy appeared to share her fascination, his gaze roving. "I haven't seen a place like this in all of Philadelphia."

His limited view of the world still tickled her. "That's why I told you the other night you should use your retirement to do some exploring. Get out of small town, USA."

"You should give it a chance. It provides its own excitement."

"Don't I know that. Chasing chickens is as exciting as outrunning a train. Neither one's for me."

"You grew up on a farm?"

They'd drawn so close in three days that she forgot she hadn't told him anything about Ned beyond his unfortunate role in her past. "My ex ran one, and I'm pretty sure he only married me to have cheap labor. Let's just say I never adapted to country life and don't have any plans to try it again."

He didn't make a reply and slid his gaze off to the side, but she detected a difference in him. His eyes lost the amused cast from when he admired their surroundings, and his movements stiffened with tension. She worried her being divorced bothered him more now that they shared a deeper bond. Maybe her remarks made him question whether she had good reason to leave Ned. She contemplated how to handle it, but their long-awaited waitress arrived with menus and took their drink orders, ending the awkward moment.

For once, their choices didn't align, with him asking for the beef tips and her wanting the flaked turkey. Even so, he agreed to take her up on her suggestion to try a peppermint sundae for dessert, which, as she told him, was topped with hot fudge and real whipped cream. The talk of the dish seemed to lighten his mood, relieving her. If sweets alone could keep him content, she didn't doubt their compatibility.

His upbeat demeanor continued during the meal, but she noticed his agitation return after he finished his ice cream. She guessed the bill daunted him, already wondering how much his trip could've netted him in light of everything they'd done. She hoped more lay behind his distance than his finances and that he was contending with the same anguish plaguing her.

When he delayed in requesting the check, she wanted to offer, yet again, to go Dutch. Her experience deterred her, as she feared it would insult him. She observed him with keen interest when the waitress handed him the bill and informed them the restaurant would close in twenty minutes. His neck expanded in a deep swallow, and she couldn't contain her guilt any longer.

"I'm sorry if you're leaving town poorer than when

you came because of me."

His eyes softened, locking with hers. "You couldn't have that more wrong; I'm leaving wealthier because of you."

Her soul danced with elation. "Our few days together have enriched me, too. I can't even tell you how much."

He leaned across the table to grasp her hand. "I'm pretty certain I already know, which leads me to another reason why I brought you here. I've lived a rather bleak life back home since I lost my wife, and I accepted—actually aimed for—it to be that way. As I saw it, I'd shared a deeper love than I could've asked for, and how could I expect more? So few find that kind of fulfillment once in a lifetime, and I figured I had to accept my turn was over. I hoped my loss somehow balanced out another's gain in the universe."

She nodded, having adopted a similar mindset in the months after Clark's sudden death.

He continued, "I'd like to claim the philosophy helped my attitude, but it didn't. I've never confessed this to anybody, but I realized I pushed my son to move far away. I don't blame him for it in the least, because he probably figured he wouldn't find happiness around a dad like me. That said, I feared what it might cost me if I continued down this foolish path of martyrdom and isolation.

"Then, I called the local operator a couple of days ago, and everything changed. Things began to matter to me again instead of blending into the dull gray backdrop of my world. I've been living, not merely existing, and I owe that to you."

Tears started to cloud her vision. "Someone

recently asked me if I'd given up on love. I didn't want to admit it, but you've helped me to realize I had. I let my failed marriage shut my mind and heart to the notion, but you've coerced me to reconsider that stance."

"I'm thankful to hear that." He winked. "A part of me hates the fact that right when I've started to embrace feeling emotions again, I have to face the pain of leaving you. Having you in my life has given me joy I didn't think the world would grace me with a second time. I've become a better man and even a better father because of it. I spoke with my son today, and we talked for longer than we have in too long. I can't leave that behind. I can't leave you behind."

To Mabel's astonishment, he stood, rounded the table, and bent down on one knee.

"So, please, don't make me." He took a diamond ring out of his coat pocket. "Be my wife, and come home with me."

Chapter Six

As she sauntered down the sidewalk, Mabel couldn't understand her own actions. She received two marriage proposals before and realized she ought to make a verbal response of some sort, not dash away in silence like this. Nonetheless, she couldn't gather her thoughts quickly enough to do much else. Her feelings for Roy ran too deep to straight up refuse his proposal, she also couldn't accept it on a whim.

Roy hustled outdoors on her tail. "Honey, wait up. I'm sorry if I pressured you too much again."

His plea halted her steps, but she still couldn't form a reply.

He took full advantage of her sudden stop, wasting no time to race to her side. "I don't make rash moves like this, but with you, I get carried away. That shows you how you've changed me. You give me this drive and spontaneity no one has ever brought out of me, except for Heidi. I love you and don't want to go back to my life without you, but if you don't feel the same, I'll accept that."

She couldn't lie and tell him she didn't return his love, but admitting it would only worsen matters. Out of desperation, she spun the spotlight on him. "Would you consider moving here? That'd be spontaneous."

Cornered, he cropped his head. "I couldn't until I retire. At my age, I can't justify starting over from scratch."

"Sad to say, I'm with you there. Evelyn needs me now more than she did when I moved in with her, and I can't abandon her after everything she's done for me."

"Do you suppose she might agree to relocate? I have a guest room I'd be thrilled to set up for her."

His kind offer and tender expression weakened her conviction, but she refused to show that. "Her son and grandchildren live near Jackson and don't get to visit her more than a few times a year as it is. I can't ask her to venture that far away."

She wondered if he'd suggest Evelyn's family take better care of her, a sentiment she grappled with on occasion, but he didn't assume the position. Instead, he seemed to concede to reality. "I understand. I didn't mean to make you uncomfortable. I should've enjoyed our evening for what it was, but I wouldn't have forgiven my lips for not telling you the way I feel. I hope I didn't hurt you."

In truth, he did but not by proposing to her. Observing his heartbreak stabbed her right down to her soul. "You didn't. I'll always cherish this week we shared. Nothing can mar that."

"I will, too." He kissed her cheek. "You'll ride home with me, won't you?"

She nodded, allowing him to wrap his arm around her as they ambled to the truck. Neither spoke much along the short journey, and despite what she told him, it saddened Mabel that their romance would end on the tainted note. Even so, her two marriages taught her she'd rather suffer the pain of losing a great love than experience the glee of parting from a miserable one.

When he drew up to the house, she failed to find

the words that would constitute a suitable send-off. She yearned to reveal her love for him, but it seemed pointless. How could she claim to love him if she refused to sacrifice her independence to be with him? At the same time, she couldn't give him the simple goodbye she would extend to a mere acquaintance.

Before she could formulate anything, Roy plucked out the ring he'd presented to her. "I bought this for you, and I don't intend to give it to anyone else. If you're ever inclined and able to accept it, I'll be ready to put it on you."

She swallowed the lump in her throat to give him one last smile. "I'll be sure to call you…if you trust me to manage that."

He grinned, but it didn't meet his eyes like usual. He tilted his head and kissed her, making her question how she could bear to let him go.

****

Like the previous night, Mabel hoped to elude Evelyn's curiosity. She doubted the hours until morning would give her the clarity to discuss Roy's proposal, but she would've appreciated it. When the illuminated living room indicated she wouldn't get it, she mentally prepared for the unavoidable conversation.

Her friend eyed her from her chair, putting aside her book. "Well, how'd the hoedown go?"

"He took me to the Greed Gala." She coined the nickname after Millie's engagement party.

"I wouldn't have guessed those rich snobs could square dance." She patted the seat beside her to prod Mabel to sit. "He must've wanted to give you both a special time. Tell me about it."

Everything before Roy's proposal evaporated from

her mind, but she sifted through her thoughts for a gem...apart from the actual gem. "My turkey was so tender, and the sundae tasted delicious, as usual. I enjoyed eating it without having Millie's scrawny little friends there to scrutinize my every bite."

"How can you babble on about your food after you spent the evening with a dashing fellow who looks at you like he does? He didn't buy a brand-new suit just to take you out for turkey. Give me the real story."

She glanced down at the clutch on her lap and decided to retrieve the ring stashed in it. She displayed it to her.

"As I suspected." Evelyn admired it with a pleased smile. "He has good taste, both in women and jewelry."

"I'm sure Millie would claim hers is bigger."

"How could it not be, when it miraculously grows every time she comments on it?" She winked, the two often discussing Millie's tendency to exaggerate. "Why aren't you wearing it? I gave him the right size. You didn't eat enough to puff up your fingers, did you?"

Mabel retracted the ring from her line of sight and stuffed it back into her bag. "When did he ask you my size?"

"After he dropped you off at work. He surprised me when he returned, but once he mentioned that, I figured it out. To tell you the truth, I'm also convinced he hoped to have another cookie, but I admitted you finished them."

She chose not to scold her for her dishonesty, armed with a different charge to level at her. "Why didn't you warn me?"

"Warn you? You warn someone of a twister coming, not an engagement. I'm sorry I didn't, now that

I see how you gorged so much that you swelled."

"I did not." She stood in anger. "I'm not wearing the ring because I didn't accept Roy's proposal. I wish you would've realized I couldn't and talked him out of it."

"What would've given me that impression? I can see you love him. Why would I anticipate anything less than you agreeing to marry him without hesitation?"

She folded her arms. "Because you understand what I've been through."

"Indeed I do, which is the reason his question made me ecstatic all day. I didn't eat much of my supper because of my excitement."

"Are you sure it had nothing to do with your feasting on my cookies the whole night?" If she could goad her on her diet, Mabel wouldn't hold back from returning it in kind.

The jab didn't veer Evelyn away from the topic of conversation. "Roy gives you the happiness you deserve and haven't had for far too long. Why wouldn't you want to marry him?"

"For one thing, I have an obligation to you, and—"

"Don't you pin this on me. I've always told you not to think you're beholden to me. I have a son and lazy daughter-in-law who shoulder that duty, and I'm more than ready to remind them of it. I didn't invite you to live here under the condition that you give up your life."

Having anticipated the reply, she lowered her eyes and searched for an explanation Evelyn would believe. "I didn't mean it as a personal affront to him. I'm past the age of thinking a husband is the prize of a woman's life, that's all."

Evelyn gave her a penetrating look. "So, you don't consider Clark a prize anymore?"

"I certainly do but not because he married me. His qualities made him a treasure."

"The same doesn't go for Roy?" She cornered Mabel.

She formed her lips to say she couldn't tell after such a short time, but she expected Evelyn to draw the comparison to her first week with Clark, like Millie did. Out of rebuttals and energy, she headed toward the stairs. "No matter what, I'm thankful to have met him and for our moments together."

Evelyn picked up her book, shaking her head. "And they all lived miserably ever after."

She ignored her until an insignificant tidbit from their squabble caught her interest. "How did you guess my ring size?"

"I didn't. I grabbed one of the cheap ones from your jewelry box and let him take it to the store. I told him not to bother returning it, seeing as you two would be married before long. Guess you'll have to call him and take him up on his proposal if you want it back."

"While I'm at it, I'll thank him for turning my roommate into a conspirator and thief."

****

Lying in bed, Mabel flipped over and squinted to read her alarm clock in the darkness. She discovered forty whole minutes had elapsed since she last checked it, a record for her that night. She couldn't recall the last time she battled insomnia like this, but she didn't doubt a man inflicted it on her. Apart from the previous evening, she floated all week on a cloud of reminders of how nice having a companion could be. Now she fell on the hard floor of the heartache that accompanied it.

She shouldn't have believed it would result in any other outcome, with her attraction to Roy so immediate and strong. She trusted her experience and constitution would shield her from human nature, rationalizing she overcame those desires in her time alone. She also didn't count on Roy to measure up to her high standards, which she hadn't held Ned to until it was too late.

In her reflection, she realized she never shut out the concept of love, but she ruled out finding anyone worthy of hers. Over the years, she resented her own hastiness in her pursuit of Ned and how she put Clark's mantle on him from the start of their relationship. While under his charming spell, she zeroed in on the most minor of similarities between the two. She concluded he could give her the same happiness as her first husband. When he didn't, it soured her on the possibility that love would ever hand her someone like Clark again.

She bucked against falling right back into that same pattern of nostalgia with Roy. She supposed her resolve to fight it incited her to take it out on him. From this point forward, she resolved not to compare others to him again, deeming it unfair. Still, she couldn't judge Roy's suitability off of a few days, even if she did with Clark. Plus, the matter of moving so far away added to the risk. Irvington, a mere twenty-five miles from home, kept her isolated from everyone, robbing her of any support through her rotten marriage. She couldn't take that chance and be hours away, to boot.

By the time the rays of dawn filtered in through her curtains, her sorrow lingered, but her confidence in her choice strengthened. If Roy lived closer, maybe they could've worked it out. Under these circumstances, they should keep their relationship confined to the memories they made. If she never dated another man after him, at least he showed her the devotion she craved.

When she rose to begin her day, her willpower faltered a bit upon spotting her jewelry box and remembering Evelyn's sneaking into it for Roy. He didn't confess it or mention the need to return it, no doubt too preoccupied with her rejection. She wondered if he'd realize his slip before he set out of town. Despite her unwavering resolution, her heart leaped at the prospect of seeing him one more time. She considered calling the hotel to catch him and use it as an excuse, but she resisted for fear of appearing selfish and hurting him further. Besides, she never wore the few rings she owned anymore.

Suspense plagued her throughout the morning, with her attention continuing to slide to the clock. At work, she kept waiting for a call from his motel or to hear from home that he dropped it off for her, but she received neither. With waning hope, she could only imagine him driving out of Louisville, then the state, and in the end, her life.

Against her better judgement, she asked Evelyn after work if he stopped over, not wanting to give her the opportunity to hide it from her. Evelyn reported he didn't show up or call, adding, "Since he let you hold on to his ring, shouldn't he be entitled to yours? It doesn't make for a very even trade, in my estimation."

Her candor didn't upset Mabel, but she didn't find humor in it, either. The sentiment ushered in emptiness, which crowded out both her heartbreak and anxious anticipation. She retreated to her bedroom in a daze. After changing out of her clothes, she picked up her clutch from off her armchair to put it back where it belonged in her closet. Before she set it on its shelf, she gave into her urge to slide out the ring once more.

At the restaurant and in the living room with Evelyn, she didn't give it more than a glance, concluding she didn't deserve the privilege to study it. In the solitude, she relented, clasping the silver band between her fingers. Four small diamonds crowned it, giving it glamor despite its overall simplicity. She marveled at how well it matched his qualities and at the same time, suited her personality. A perfect fit on her hand, she wondered whether it signified the beautiful union they could make.

Uneager to get too attached, she took it off and secured it back into the bag's inner pocket. The valuable keepsake warranted a better place, but she didn't want to lose it among her other, menial possessions. She kept her most precious treasures in her memories box, but she'd long ago restricted it to hold the mementos that pertained to Clark and nothing else. The remembrance of Roy merited its own honorable spot, yet she couldn't muster the fortitude to designate one.

She did her best to steer her thoughts away from him, but the void inside of her deepened by the hour. Waves of expectation washed over her at random moments, as she remained somewhat hopeful he'd call to inform her of his safe arrival in Coatesville. Given her failure to request the update, she didn't fret over the lack thereof, but his silence underscored the growing distance between them.

Widening the gap, he didn't offer her his phone number when he took hers. Of course, she could obtain it, but the traditional side of her didn't deem it appropriate to do so. She preferred to wait on to him to make contact if he wished, never one to force herself on a guy. Besides that, she figured she shouldn't infringe on him if he needed space when she pushed him away in the first place.

Saturday morning, she focused on returning to the life she led six days prior, which, in her opinion, wasn't so bad. To her gratitude, Evelyn reminded her about the commitment she made to take Bev to the ballgame, and despite her initial reluctance, she welcomed the distraction. A part of her worried her niece would mention Roy, but she rationalized the girl would care too much about her own fling to give any attention to her aunt's.

She proved Mabel wrong the second she boarded the bus and sat down beside her, her eyes big above her cheesy grin.

"So, how'd you enjoy Fountaine Ferry?"

The excursion seemed like a lifetime ago. "I had fun. For your information, I rode a roller coaster."

"Mom told me. I couldn't believe it. I can't remember much from the time you went with us, but I'll never forget your argument with Mom about not going on one. She called you a baby."

She grimaced at the memory of the incident. "I still don't understand why it made her so angry. If I didn't volunteer to stay with you, she would've had to. I may be a coward, but I'm a responsible one."

"Did you like it?"

"I lived."

Her eyes twinkled with mischief. "Was it more dangerous than your car crash?"

"Your mother exaggerates. I had more of a thump than a crash." *Then why'd you go to pieces?* her conscience needled her.

Bev didn't have such a sharp turn of mind…for now, anyways. "Whatever the case, Roy must have really captivated you to get you to break out of your square that much."

"People have called me many things, my dear, but never a square."

"Well, I'm proud to be the first." She straightened her posture and puffed out her chest, revealing how much of her aunt's sass she inherited. "Do you think he'll visit again sometime? Mom and I both want to meet him."

The question tore at Mabel's heart. "I doubt it. He's wrapped up his business, and he didn't indicate he'd have to return."

"But who's to say he won't want to?" Bev winked

Mabel shook her head and peered out the window. When the girl kept quiet for a beat, she figured the subject of her love life had died, but Bev surprised her again.

"I laughed when Mom told me he coerced you to drive. That sounds like something Harold would do with me. I can't imagine old people doing that."

She shot her a piercing—but playful—glower. "But you think this old woman would want to spend her Saturday watching teenage boys take whacks at a baseball? I could be napping in a rocking chair."

Bev giggled, quicker on the take than Lorna. With

only a mile to go before their stop, their banter drew to a close. Along their walk, Mabel mulled over her niece's remark about Roy putting her behind the wheel. She still couldn't figure his reason for the stunt, nor did he give her a clear answer. She considered it a strange thing to do on what should've been his last night in town and at the late hour. She would've rather he kept to their usual repartee she so enjoyed.

That in mind, it occurred to her the problem lay there: Roy wanted more than their usual patter. If he'd started to contemplate marriage, he, like Ned, may have wanted to teach her so she could get around in a small town that didn't have buses. Ned wanted to equip her to carry out the duties of the farm, but she surmised Roy intended to further her independence for her own benefit. She appreciated such a motive, but she still resented the notion of him trying to change her.

When they arrived at the field, Bev took an open space in the front row of the bleachers, and she followed, cringing. She never could understand who thought such uncomfortable seating would enhance the experience of an already boring sport. She sucked in her chagrin, glad not to be sitting at home wallowing in her sorrows. She may not have liked baseball much, but she found entertainment in her observations. For instance, it tickled her every time the announcer referred to the players as men, when the boys on the field couldn't even grow facial hair. She also became engrossed in the pitcher's struggle to keep his oversized glove on his hand.

For her part, Bev's attention remained fixed on Harold, the team's shortstop. She shouted when he strode up to bat and cheered if he made the slightest contact with the ball. After his third strikeout, Mabel could sense her intrigue waning. She pivoted toward her aunt, making Mabel hope she'd tell her they didn't have to sit through the final inning. She couldn't be so fortunate.

"You miss him, don't you?"

"Who?" Mabel stalled.

"Roy. I can tell you're moping."

"I'm moping because of my aching rear."

The girl tilted her head in clear distrust. "I don't believe you. Come on, admit it."

Mabel obliged her to a degree. "Sure, I liked having him here, but I realized he couldn't stay."

She arched her brow, triumphant. "And that's why you went out with him, isn't it? Haven't we had this conversation before?"

She maintained her determination not to confess the impact of their exchange last week. "Someday, you'll understand how many times people enter and drift out of our lives, whether they plan to or not. Nothing's as simple as you believe it is."

"If you ask me, grownups make life so hard on themselves."

She sighed. "No, honey, experience does."

****

Riding home from the game, Mabel gazed out the window at the town's variety of attractions and couldn't keep her mind off Roy. She wished she could've shown him more landmarks and began to reconsider her choices in where she'd taken him. When she didn't view him as more than a stranger, she didn't give her recommendation a great deal of concern. She just picked a quaint place the majority of visitors overlooked. The rest of their destinations seemed to domino out of her control, and in retrospect, she regretted that. With how strong her feelings for him grew, she now would've liked to have shared more of her typical stomping grounds. They might have endeared him to the city.

Then again, she might've had a harder time returning to them without him. She already missed his presence at the house and their interaction at the phone company. No matter where they visited, he would leave an indelible mark on her heart. She longed to enjoy more time with him, even if they spent it in a vacant lot. Her conscience reminded her that he extended the opportunity to her. One little "yes" would've afforded her as much time with him as life permitted.

Grappling with her inner conflict, she stayed on the bus instead of accompanying Bev into her house. She didn't need Millie's scolding on top of everything else. She doubted she'd ever disclose Roy's proposal to anybody except Evelyn, deeming it nobody's business. She figured Millie would express an opinion similar to Evelyn's, but Mabel couldn't offer her any better answers than she gave her roommate.

She dreaded going home to continue the debate, but Evelyn surprised her by not making a single mention of Roy. Although she could be ornery, she had a knack for reading people and seemed to sense Mabel needed a reprieve from the subject. Hence she asked for some assistance in the garden, after which she enlisted her help with the day's crossword puzzle in the newspaper.

"This one should be easy for you. A word with four letters that describes what a phone does. I thought 'call,' but it ends in *G*."

Mabel considered it from her seat on the back porch. "Could it be *ring*?"

"Oh, of course." A few minutes later, she acted stumped again. "A five-letter word that's the opposite of groom. It isn't *dirty* because it starts with a *B*."

"Maybe *bride*."

She giggled in innocence. "Silly me. I guess I'm more used to grooming dogs than I am the other sort of groom. What would a seven-letter synonym for accident be? It has a *T* and a *K* in it."

It took Mabel a moment, but she succeeded once more. "*Mistake*."

Evelyn thanked her before Mabel put the three together—ring, bride, and mistake—and solved the real riddle at play. She extended her hand. "Let me see if I can figure out any others for you."

"I have everything now, but I appreciate your offer." She kept a firm hold on it and scampered inside. Mabel assumed she'd destroy the evidence that the puzzle didn't present any of those clues.

Mabel dropped the matter, uneager to start the dispute she managed to avoid all day.

Sunday dragged on like the last two days, but by the evening, she accepted Roy wouldn't call. He returned to his life, and she should, too. As she washed the dishes and checked the clock, she realized the moment marked a week since her innocent back-and-forth with Bev on the bus. A lot happened in the short span of time, but at the core of the matter, how much had changed? She reverted to her tendency of keeping her distance from a real relationship, even at the cost of true love. The realization shamed her because of how much Roy allowed her to transform him, when she wouldn't evolve along with him.

Reporting to work Monday, she determined to pretend like the week before didn't mean as much as it did. With Lorna on her honeymoon, she wouldn't have to face her until she ventured home. Despite how the girl's over-the-top bliss sickened her, she hoped the trip would distract her from her *old* coworker's brush with romance. She still had to deal with Georgette, who she steered clear of on Friday, but realized she couldn't avoid for much longer.

Living up to Mabel's expectations, Georgette awaited her at her locker, curiosity all over her face.

"Morning." Mabel remained nonchalant. "Did you enjoy your weekend?"

"Sure did, but one look at you tells me you can't say the same."

"Why? Do I appear to have gone mute?"

Georgette didn't acknowledge the wry remark. "I take it lover boy headed back north."

"Oh, that Stentz fella? Yeah, he took off on Friday. I'd imagine he's punching in at his factory right now."

"So he's called you?"

"Why should he? I showed him around town, but that's as far as it went."

She shook her head. "You and I both know that isn't the least bit true. I sensed how smitten you were, and I could hear the enchantment in his voice after just two dates. I don't believe for a second that he dropped you cold."

Mabel didn't owe her an explanation, so she neglected to give her one. "How'd Lorna's wedding go? Did they have to recite the vows to her word by word?"

"No, she wrote her own."

A genuine smile crossed her lips for the first time in four days. "If she'd told me that, I would've agreed to go without hesitation."

Georgette wrinkled her chin, not appearing angry but sad. "I don't know what happened between you and Roy, and I'm not asking you to tell me. All I can say is I've never observed you as happy as you seemed last week, and I enjoyed it. You deserve it, even if you can't admit it."

She nodded and tried to thank her for the sentiment, but the lump in her throat caught her words. She drew a deep breath to say she needed to go to the restroom before their shift began.

Once inside the stall, she wept until her eyes couldn't release any more tears.

Chapter Seven

Mabel spent the majority of her week adjusting to her life without Roy. Her need to do so frustrated her, considering it was her normal routine, and he'd been the variable for four days. Why should she have to get accustomed to her usual? How could she become this entangled in a man again?

Without giving it much thought, she busied her nights in housework, taking on a variety of odd jobs. Evelyn called her out on it, given Mabel convinced her they could skip many of them when they did their spring cleaning.

"I see. You'll clean out my cupboards if it's on your terms."

Mabel ignored the razzing but questioned the reason behind her sudden inspiration. During one of her breaks, she combed through her mind and pinpointed the last time she was this occupied.

****

The ten days after Clark returned home inched by, seeming like every bit of five years in Mabel's world. The hours crawled at both work and home, with her new responsibilities taxing her unlike anything she took on before. Her mother needed her help for tasks big and small, keeping her busy from the time she awoke to the moment she collapsed into bed. Her usually kind mother also made frequent complaints about the way

Mabel tended to her concerns, which added to the pressure. She endeavored to show her understanding, aware her frustration stemmed from her distress over the circumstances, but the words still held the power to stab her.

Millie's school granted her the provision to finish the year from home, allowing her to care for Mom while Mabel worked. To supplement her paycheck from the telephone company, she secured a job waiting tables at a bistro in the evenings. She never arrived home sooner than eleven and always found chores awaiting her before she could sleep. On the first night she cried, aware she wouldn't be able to live single-mindedly again.

With their second weekend nearing its end, she caught up on the rest of her housework so she could start the week with a clean slate. She managed to sit down to relax around nine o'clock, when Saturday's mail beckoned to her from the desk beside her. She cringed, hating to sift through the stream of sympathy cards and other paperwork concerning her dad's death. Since she didn't want to have a double-sized stack to rifle through Monday, she grabbed it with a sigh.

She found much of the same, with the addition of a bill from the hospital in Chicago. The document made her nauseous, both because of the memory of the accident and their troubled finances. Underneath it, another envelope lay with a return address in Chicago. She started to toss it aside with the bill, but upon spotting Clark's name, she tore it open without delay.

Dearest Mabel,

I'm sorry I haven't kept to my own request to write, but please don't take my delay to mean I haven't been thinking of you. On the contrary, you play through my mind from the instant I rise regardless of where I am. Every time I have to work on the pool, my eyes linger on the chair you sat in the day we met, wishing to find the beauty I did then.

Ever since I left you, I've struggled to figure out how to express the way I feel. You carry such a heavy load, and I wouldn't want to make it worse by regaling you with how much I miss you. I imagine what you're doing throughout the day, which gives me a combination of pride, sorrow, and anxiety all at once. Your incredible family impressed me from the time we first ate together, but my appreciation grows more by the day. I can't even fathom what pride your mom must have in you for the sacrifice and care you're displaying to her and Millie.

I want to ease your burden somehow, and like I said, that held me back from penning this because nothing I can tell you seems adequate. Still, I hope the knowledge that I hold you in my mind and heart at every moment gives you a measure of peace.

All My Love,

Clark

Tears cascaded down her face as she read it over twice more, but for the first time in weeks, she smiled.

****

Reflecting on the months after her dad's death and Clark's departure, she identified how much her duties back then helped her cope with her losses, despite the toll they took on her. She rationalized she reverted to the mechanism to overcome her present despair. She didn't voice the epiphany, wanting to downplay her private turmoil, especially to Evelyn.

When Saturday arrived, she broke with her standards for fashion and dug out her lone pair of jeans for the dirty work she planned. Before the heat of the day peaked, she weeded the flower beds and garden, one of her least favorite jobs due to her morbid fear of snakes. No slithery beasts greeted her this time, giving her the impetus to complete her other dreaded to-dos, like cleaning the ash marks out of the fireplace. Evelyn approached her while she scrubbed away and dangled a piece of mail in front of her.

Mabel didn't pay it any attention. "You can set it on my chair for me to read later."

Mabel had her back turned to her, but she could hear the delight in Evelyn's voice. "I'm not sure you want to wait. It's addressed from Coatesville, Pennsylvania."

Her stubbornness wouldn't allow her to show her eagerness. "I have my hands full and will have to wash them before I touch anything. I'll get to it when I can."

Evelyn let out a tsk and clicked her heels out of the room. Mabel continued with her task while her meddlesome friend stuck around, but once alone, she bolted over to grab the envelope. Not caring about the marks her filthy fingers would leave, she ripped it open with zeal, taking in Roy's neat handwriting. In the upper right corner, he dated it as Tuesday night at nine-thirty, his precision tickling her.

Hello Mabel,

After much debate, I've sat down to write this, hoping it won't trouble you. Ever since we parted, I've beaten myself up over the unfair position I put you in the last night we spent together. Every moment with you gave me such joy, and I should've embraced that while

I could, instead of succumbing to my selfish desire not to let it end.

I don't regret my offer or the vulnerability I manifested, as both are still yours for the taking. Rather, I hate how I wiped your pretty smile off of your face and took away the contagious laughter my ears cherish to hear. I love your bright soul and would never want to dim it, even for a second. Please forgive me if I did.

Everything I told you at the restaurant holds true, and returning home to a life without you has been the dreary pit I expected. I'm not blaming you for it or begging you to change your mind. All the same, I'd like to ask if you'd allow me to keep in touch with you, if it wouldn't bother you, that is. You make me a better person, and regardless of how our time together may have concluded, I don't want to lose you for good. You're welcome to write me back or call me at the number below. I trust you'll dial correctly sooner or later.

Only Yours,

Roy

The words touched her, conveying care Ned once convinced her she didn't deserve. She appreciated the knowledge that Roy, too, struggled to dismiss thoughts of their relationship. The humor in his conclusion also warmed her heart, proving how well he understood her jovial spirit and how he complemented it.

As much as she wanted to rush to the phone, she couldn't suppress her underlying remorse. His enduring affection and mercy soothed some of her guilt, but she couldn't keep hurting him with continued contact. While he may not plan to persuade her to reconsider their future, his desire for it may well grow, provided they remain on good terms. She feared hers would, too, but she wouldn't compromise her position. Like she anticipated of their short-lived rendezvous, their maintaining contact couldn't lead to anything but heartbreak.

For self-preservation, she sought to conceal the note from her sight and from Evelyn's reach. She hovered it over the trash bag she kept nearby during her tidying fit, but to toss out such beautiful expressions didn't sit right with her. She tiptoed up to her room to stash it away somewhere quick but couldn't choose the proper place. She hesitated, her gaze again shifting toward her memories box, but she reaffirmed her resolve to keep it reserved to her keepsakes from Clark. Instead, she opted to secure it in her clutch, alongside the ring.

She returned to her cleaning and waited for Evelyn to ask about it. To her surprise, she didn't yield to the curiosity painted across her face. Mabel appreciated her kind consideration, uncertain of what she'd even say. More than that, her insight into what Evelyn would fire back daunted her. She already made too many logical points in their past discussions, and Mabel didn't want to give her another chance to sway her.

By Sunday evening, she assessed her work and realized she'd completed her sweep of the house, unless she coerced Evelyn to do a full-on renovation. Her heart sank a little, as it forced her to confront everything her escape mission enabled her to avoid. A new week awaited her, but she didn't anticipate new possibilities. She faced the same ol', same ol', and she again hated how the notion bothered her. What she once accepted and even enjoyed now glared at her like an enemy.

She cast it out of her thoughts and determined she'd get back into her groove before long. With the exception of Clark, she never pined over a guy for an extended period, and she wouldn't start this late in life. After all, she'd learned better than to rest her happiness on someone else's shoulders. Even so, her mind wandered farther into the future, and it struck her that she couldn't envision much of one, unless she added Roy to it.

In a haze, she carried out her regular Monday morning routine, landing back at work with minimal effort. She didn't hurry to put away her pocketbook, not scheduled to report to her station for ten minutes. Her lack of initiative cost her, with Lorna waltzing in the door and almost blinding her with her newlywed glow.

"Morning, all," she greeted the group of five women. "What'd I miss while my husband pampered me in Bermuda?"

Mabel chided at the question, which didn't concern anyone but Lorna alone. Uninterested in pandering to her, she scrammed out of the room, throwing it on the others around to step in and patronize the girl. To her disappointment, they seemed to share her reluctance, which caused the desperate bride to rush to her side.

"What's new, Mabel?"

She wanted to suggest she should change her technique of getting attention, but she decided to go easy on her. "I'd say you're the one with the news, Mrs…"

"Nickerson. Lorna Nickerson—I'll never tire of hearing that."

"Did the Nickersons have a nice honeymoon?"

"Oh, yes, we had a wonderful time! I'd never seen the ocean before in my life, and I couldn't believe how gorgeous it was. When I told Harold that, he said that's how he felt about me when we met. Isn't he sweet?"

Mabel nodded, encouraging Lorna to babble on about her trip for the next five minutes. When they entered the cord board room, she quickened her speech so she could fit in everything she wanted to share. She didn't even sit down at her station when they approached it. She prattled on until she seemed to recognize her failure to show any interest in her colleague beyond her first query.

"How are things going with you and your man? Will we be having another wedding soon?"

The image of Roy on his knee drifted into her mind's eye. "No, I don't think so. He's back to his life, and I'm here with mine."

"That's a shame. I told Harold on our flight home we need to embrace this time in our lives because it doesn't last forever. Some people never find love, so we have to appreciate it if we do."

Mabel offered a simple nod in response, but for once, Lorna's words did more than irritate her.

****

Dear Roy,

Thank you for writing me. After you left, I discovered I didn't have any of your information and wondered if that was your idea of an effective getaway. I considered calling the out-of-town operator, but like you, I've learned you can't always depend on them.

I, too, am sorry for the way your trip ended and realize I carry most of the blame for it. No use in arguing about it; it's true. From the moment I spotted

127

you on our first date, I had a hunch we wouldn't enjoy saying goodbye. Perhaps my reluctance to do so drove me to lash out at you on both of our final dates, in hopes it wouldn't hurt as much if we parted on bad terms.

Whatever my reasoning, I understand now how foolish it was. My choice remains the same, but I regret the way I presented it and most of all, the pain it caused you. I wouldn't have blamed you for ripping up my information and never thinking of me again. I appreciate your forgiveness.

If I still bring you happiness, feel free to write back. I miss you, too.

Mabel

She sat and reread her words, picking up her pen to change a few here and there. She paused before proceeding, not wanting to make a mess of this draft like she did the three before it. Still, she scrutinized each syllable to assess if it conveyed the right message but soon figured out she didn't understand her own intentions. Just the same, she couldn't quell her longing to reach out ever since Lorna's statement that morning.

She tore the paper off her writing tablet and scanned through it for another moment, mulling it over before she committed to folding it.

Evelyn sneered at her from her chair. "Good grief. Would you send it and be done with it already?"

"Your book must be pretty boring if you're more riveted by me than it."

"How do you expect me to be able to concentrate amidst your constant groaning, pen slashing, and crumpling paper?"

Mabel shot her a pointed look. With exaggerated

movements, she proceeded to double it and stuff it into the envelope.

She gave her a daring grin. "You won't convince me until you stamp it."

Mabel marched to the desk and retrieved a postage book to counter the challenge. Five minutes later, she had it addressed and in the mailbox. Once inside, she marched up the stairs to her room, her gait triumphant.

Sprawling out onto her bed, she closed her eyes under the weight of her hidden exhaustion. She may have put on an animated act for Evelyn, but in truth, the whole day took its toll on her. She spent every moment fixated on what she would and wouldn't say to Roy, making it a struggle to focus on her work. She caught her slips just in time to avert an incident, not ready to repeat what happened when Roy first called.

Regardless of her personal feelings toward Lorna, she needed her comment about how one should treasure finding love. Although the young woman's misconceptions about age tainted it a bit, the sentiment reminded her she should look beyond her rigid standards. While she couldn't follow him home like he asked, she loved him and wanted to show that. While she feared keeping in contact with him would hurt them both in the long run, she realized ignoring him would cut him to the heart, too. She could hope he'd forget her and find someone else, but she didn't have any control over that. She could only retain a vestige of their relationship now or walk away from it forever.

The simple note didn't seem like much, but it filled her with tension for the rest of the week. She kept wondering when he'd receive it and what impression he would get from it. Calling him, of course, would've spared her the suspense, but the notion still intimidated her. His voice held the power to break down her defenses, which landed her in this predicament in the first place.

On Saturday yet again, she received his response at last. Unlike his previous letter, this one carried a lighter tone, not referencing their estrangement at all. He assured her that her reply made him *as happy as a sunflower*, and he gave a casual report of his week. He shared the house projects he started, like installing a new water heater and renovating a closet. She surmised he used it all as a distraction technique like she did in the days after his departure. She used the similarity to her advantage, recounting some of the improvements she made to the townhouse in her follow-up.

Her apprehension eased with each note she wrote to him, and she could sense his guard lowering as time passed, too. By the month's end, they swapped letters almost every day, and on the rare occasions she didn't find one, two arrived the next day. Aside from his few offhand remarks about what he planned to show her if she ever visited him, they pretty much stuck to their ordinary goings-on. Still, she couldn't dispose of them and kept storing them away in her clutch, which grew more and more difficult to close.

When Roy asked for a picture of her, she hesitated, as the small request signaled a bigger commitment. He mentioned it after he related a story involving his friends, so she figured he told them about her, too, and wanted to show it around. Along with that, she supposed he could want a reminder of her to look at nearby. In all honesty, she wished she had one of him and regretted not having one taken of them during his stay. Nonetheless, her doubts over their future crept back. She didn't want to ignite his hopes of her rethinking his proposal.

She compromised, obliging him while not giving in to her own urge to elicit one in return. He didn't volunteer it, not the self-assuming type, but he showed courage in taking the initiative to jolt her out of her comfort zone again. A month into their pen pal arrangement, the telephone rang on a Wednesday evening. Contrary to the attention she had to give to her exchanges at work, she answered with her mind preoccupied with washing the last of the dishes.

"Hello?"

"Aren't you going ask, *To whom am I speaking?*" She could envision Roy's smile, and it made her melt inside.

"To whom am I speaking, Mr. Stentz, and what line shall I fail to transfer you to today?" She humored him, and all of a sudden, Evelyn shuffled into the room with wide eyes.

He snickered. "There's the voice I've missed so much. I sat down to write you but spotted the phone and took a chance. I hope you don't mind."

Her pulse racing, she couldn't claim the surprise didn't unnerve her, but his joviality made it impossible for her to manifest anything other than joy. "No, sir. I'm glad to hear from you. It's déjà vu. The other day, someone called from the hotel where you stayed, and it disappointed me when it wasn't you."

"You didn't go out on a date with him, did you?"

His playful threat gave her a charge. "He didn't invite me on one. I guess I don't cast the same appeal when I do my job right."

"Well, keep up the good work. How's Evelyn?"

"She's nosey but fine." Mabel stared right at her friend as she made the remark. "I can't say if she has a stronger craving for the cookies we made when you visited or for a peek at your letters."

"You ought to give her a little of each once in a while."

"A little? She's finished three pans since you headed home."

Evelyn scowled at her.

"Do you think you could send one my way?" Roy inquired.

"I doubt it'd survive the journey."

"I do, too. A postal worker is liable to break into the package the instant he smells it. I'll have to drive down there for another taste."

Hope budded in her heart. "I reckon so."

"Unless you want to bring it with you when you visit me." His words teemed with charisma.

Mabel admired his cunning. "Slow down, Mr. Stentz."

****

Over the course of the next few weeks, Mabel and Roy talked on the phone most nights, crowding out the usual time they set aside to write each other. Thus, their letters dried up to a large degree, but they drew closer than ever. They shared deep conversations at first, but after a while, they switched to lighter, everyday subjects like in their notes. They even watched variety shows during their chats so they could exchange opinions on the acts. More and more, it reminded her of how much she enjoyed having that kind of regular companionship with a man who loved and valued her.

Though it rang up both their phone bills, their routine gave her the satisfaction that they could have a life together of sorts, despite the miles between them. She still missed him, and he voiced that he did her, too. He continued to throw out hints about her visiting and referenced marriage a couple of times, but he never sounded desperate or downhearted. Her guilt for refusing his proposal abated, as she no longer pictured him moping around because of her.

He called earlier than normal one Sunday evening, interrupting her popcorn-making. She didn't mind, except for the fact that she struggled to hear him over the volume of the popping kernels. Given their tradition of collaborating their choice of snack, she concluded he would tell her he craved something different.

She forewent the preamble. "You can opt for potato chips, but I'm sticking with my popcorn."

"I'm too excited to eat, honey. I spoke with Gregory tonight, and my prediction proved true: I'm going to be a grandfather!"

"Oh, Roy, that's wonderful. I'll bet they're thrilled."

"Thrilled and terrified all at the same time, as they should be." He chuckled.

"Congratulations, Grandpa Roy."

"I appreciate it, but boy, does that sound strange. To be honest, I think I prefer Grampy. That's what I called my mother's dad."

"Grampy Roy—that does have a nice ring to it. When is the little one due to arrive?"

"February. They didn't waste any time. They married in April."

"That's pretty much what happened to Clark and

me," she mused without thinking.

"What do you mean? Didn't you say you never had children?"

"We didn't." Her whole body tightened, accustomed to blocking out the memory. He didn't speak, obviously waiting for more of an explanation. With her stomach in a knot and her mouth dry, she considered claiming to have misspoken, but she doubted he'd believe it.

"I found out I was pregnant soon after we returned home from our honeymoon. We didn't want a baby right away since we lived with my mom, but we were tickled regardless. Everything seemed fine until I developed a fever in my fourth month and ended up suffering a miscarriage. The next year, the same thing happened but earlier along. My doctor couldn't tell us why, but I couldn't get pregnant again. Up to the day I lost Clark, we hoped to have a child of our own sooner or later."

Roy sighed. "That's tragic. I'm so sorry."

"Thank you. I'm sorry to spoil your celebration. I didn't plan to mention it. I guess I get too comfortable talking to you."

"That's all right with me, sweetie. I just wish I could act as more than a listening piece. I'd love to wrap you in my arms right now."

"I'd take that, too," she admitted, but her nerves tensed with the insight into where the conversation may lead. In an effort to prevent it, she circled back to the subject of his grandchild on the way. "Do you think you'll head down there for the birth?"

"I hope to go within the first few weeks if the weather and my son allow me. Would you care to join me for the ride?"

She smirked at his powers of persuasion. "I wouldn't mind, but I'd call that a family moment."

"And I'm convinced you'll be part of our family someday. *Grandma Mabel* sounds nice to me."

The title struck her as utterly foreign, having never considered such a concept in her future. "After hearing about my various calamities, I'd expect you to write me off as a jinx and want to keep your distance. You even experienced it first-hand when you let me drive."

"You couldn't be more wrong. I see a woman I love who deserves some long overdue happiness, and I want to give it to her."

His sentiment planted a lump in her throat. "You already have."

"Not like I would if you'd let me." His soft words poured out with tenderness traced with pain.

****

When their favorite show started, Mabel and Roy fell into their typical patter, sharing their thoughts on the featured performers. At the same time, a constraint lay deep inside her in the wake of her confession about her miscarriages, and she sensed something similar in Roy. She doubted his strain pertained as much to her past as it did her future. She figured he would've liked a more favorable response to his remarks about her joining his family and his desire to make her happy. Deep down, she hated herself for not giving it to him.

The unspoken friction ushered in the reservations she'd rather ignore over their continued contact. From the disappointment in his voice, she discerned the arrangement didn't suffice for him, even if she wanted to believe it did. She figured his discontent would only grow as time passed, and she couldn't decide how best to deal with that. She hated to drop him cold, but it didn't seem fair to allow them to fall deeper in love if she wouldn't concede to his wishes.

Not helping her unrest, Evelyn gave her take on their conversation the next day at breakfast. "For someone you don't want to marry, you sure share a lot with Roy."

She didn't want to start the week off with an argument, so she resorted to humor. "You should hear what I tell him after you go to bed."

"I do. I listen from the top of the staircase until you hang up the phone. After all, I pay half the bill. Shouldn't I get something out of it?"

"Rest assured, I intend to fork over the whole amount this month, so you're welcome to call whoever you want. I won't even eavesdrop," Mabel replied.

"How generous of you. Is that why you cut your conversation short last night?"

"It wasn't any shorter than normal."

"Not if you measure the minutes, but it was pretty small on content. From this side, it seemed like Roy did most of the talking," Evelyn said.

Mabel stood to wash out her cereal bowl. "Well, I'm sorry if it disappointed you not to glean much juice."

Evelyn grasped her hand as she strode by. "I don't care about that. I'm worried about you. I understand it took a lot of strength to discuss your miscarriages."

Having lost her first baby, too, she supported Mabel through both tragedies. Over the years, she expressed her sorrow to Evelyn more than she confided in anyone else.

"I wish I didn't let it slip. I took away his joy of his new grandchild and made him want to comfort me."

"And why is that so horrible?"

"Because he thinks comforting me means marrying me, and he said he wouldn't press the issue. Plus, he doesn't need to console me. Clark did that."

Evelyn regarded her in clear surprise. Mabel kept her face steady, unwilling to acknowledge how her confession stunned even her.

"For weeks, I keep hearing how you won't allow Roy to control you like Ned did. Now, you say you don't want him to show you the love Clark used to? That isn't fair. He'd better not manifest any traits of Ned's, but he can't remind you of Clark, either? I've heard of contrary women, but you lead the pack."

She understood her logic, but she wouldn't relent. "If I'm going to start over with someone new, I expect him to be his own person."

"And he is. You're the one who insists on drawing these petty comparisons."

"They aren't petty. Speaking of *contrary women*, how can you counsel me on this when you chose not to date anybody after Vincent passed?"

Evelyn didn't bite on the fighting words. "I don't want you to rob yourself of happiness, that's all. You deserve to be more than the grieving widow or the embittered divorcee. On the same token, Roy deserves the chance to be more than someone who fits between Ned and Clark on your ridiculous measuring stick. You shouldn't put limits on your relationship based on your past. I hope you'll see that someday."

With tears welling up in her eyes, she squeezed her friend's shoulder and exited the room.

****

Mabel pondered her debate with Evelyn during her ride to work, vacillating between remorse over her actions and a reluctance to change them. She brushed off Evelyn's point about the unfair confines she placed Roy into, but she couldn't remedy the sting her words inflicted. Though she loved Roy, she had indeed blocked him from the part of her heart Clark touched. She couldn't even store her mementos of him out in the open, socking them away in her small purse in a dark corner.

Nobody deserved to be boxed in like that, but her protectiveness of Clark warred with her loyalty to Roy. After some contemplation, she realized how her unpleasant history with Ned distorted her view of Clark beyond her notice. She elevated him on a pedestal, towering it too high for anyone to climb. Meanwhile, her travails with Ned heightened her awareness of what she didn't like in a man, which also impacted her perspective of others. Whether she wanted to admit it or not, she did allow her past to govern her present and future.

Approaching the building, she pondered the advantages of meeting Roy versus the drawbacks. Their dates and contact invigorated her more than anything had in years, and she did love him. That said, she spent the majority of her time now in self-examination, combing through the many aspects of her life she used to overlook. Some who adopted the *new age* mentality would claim such psychoanalysis benefitted her, but in reality, it made her miserable. Despite what Evelyn and Bev expressed, she didn't mind her life before Roy Stentz arrived in town. Loneliness trumped questioning her every emotion.

Once in the locker room, she determined to let up on her Freudian thoughts. Right after she secured her purse, she found a convenient distraction in the form of an old friend.

"Well, if it isn't Merry Time Mabel."

She recognized both her childhood nickname and the voice who announced it, but she whipped her head around for confirmation. "And that looks like Flirty Frances."

Frances Baxter giggled at the greeting, and the former classmates met in the middle of the room to embrace.

Once they let go of each other, Georgette joined the conversation from her nearby locker. "Merry Time Mabel? Who's she?"

Mabel shook her head over the never-ending jokes about her tamer demeanor. "This is Frances Baxter, Georgette. Frances, meet my pest of a coworker, Georgette Higgins. Frances and I attended high school together and snagged jobs here after graduation. Six months later, she ditched me to go to acting school, and a big-shot producer discovered her there. She made her stage debut before she even earned her degree."

Georgette extended her hand to Frances. "My, I didn't expect to meet a celebrity today."

"Well, give me a heads-up if you find one," Frances replied with a smile.

"What brings this award-nominated actress to our humble quarters?" Mabel enjoyed teasing her about her one and only nomination a decade prior.

"I'm staying with Mom for a week before I start rehearsals for the new production I'm in this fall. My brother told me she was getting feeble, and I'd better make the trip when I had the chance, but I think he just wanted a break." She rolled her eyes. "I've wanted to swing by ever since I landed Thursday, but she's kept me so busy, running here and there. I snuck out today before she woke up. I didn't know for certain if you'd changed jobs recently or not, but I figured I'd give it a try. I called Evelyn's a couple of times last night but couldn't get through. She must've stayed up late, gossiping."

"No, I'm afraid I was the chatterbox." Her cheeks warmed, in part because she predicted Evelyn—and no doubt Roy—would contradict the statement.

"Yeah, she and her gentleman caller talk the evenings away," Georgette murmured as she strolled past them.

She cocked her eyebrow. "Gentleman caller, huh? Dish, woman."

"I don't have much to dish. I went out a few times with a fella when he visited here on business, and we've kept in touch to a degree. Tell me more about your new show."

Her cheer faded into disgust. "It's a low-budget flop. It's based on a French play about a guy who's on his way to his wedding when his horse eats a straw hat that belongs to his ex-girlfriend. I've never hated a role so much, but I had to take something. Needless to say, you must have more to spill on your man than I do about my lousy part. Where does he live?"

"Pennsylvania. He keeps badgering me to move there, but I'm done letting a man dictate what I do. Ned taught me that lesson the hard way." She maintained her confidence, warding off her guilt from her exchange with Evelyn.

"You aren't kidding. That's the reason I never married. I'm exhausted by directors bossing me around for nine hours a day. I want control at home."

"Smart woman."

Frances glanced at the clock on the wall beside them. "I'll let you go so you're not late to your station, but I wanted to ask if you'd like to get away for the weekend? I'm going to hitch a ride back to the city with a couple of the girls. We're going to catch a show and do some shopping. There's a boutique I've always wanted you to see."

The invitation intrigued her, but her vague mention of *the girls* made Mabel think twice before accepting. "Who else is coming?"

"Helen." She glanced off to the side for a second but braved to meet Mabel's eyes as she stated the other name. "And Audrey."

Mabel didn't hesitate. "I wish I could, but I've put off a root canal for months. I'll schedule it now that I have a worse option. At least it will benefit me, unlike being trapped in a car with Audrey Detwiler."

"She's grown up, Mabel, and so should you. She's not telling everyone your breath stinks anymore."

"How can you be so sure? You live hundreds of miles away."

Frances leveled a pointed glare at her. "You're not spreading the awful rumor that she was born on a circus train anymore, are you?"

She cackled at the reminder. "I haven't shared it in a few years."

"I didn't want her to tag along, but Helen insisted. Having you would make it so much more fun."

She mulled it over, picturing the possibilities, and a refusal circled the tip of her tongue. When she reflected on her unsettled feelings from the past month, she craved a respite from it all, especially under the shimmering lights of New York City. Given what she endured in the decades after she graduated, she could survive Audrey Detwiler for three days.

"All right, you've persuaded me. I'll request Friday and Monday off, and we'll see if the boss approves it."

Frances exclaimed with glee and hugged her.

Chapter Eight

For the first time since Roy's departure, Mabel brimmed with anticipation, breaking out of her incessant quandary about her lot in life. Instead of contemplating what awaited her in twenty years, her mind revolved around what outfits she'd wear to grace bustling streets and glamorous theaters. She bought a copy of the national newspaper over her lunch hour and consulted the weather forecast to aid her planning. In truth, she wished the temperatures would dip low enough to warrant her to take the mink. To her disappointment, it didn't predict an August blizzard, but she'd scratch her itch by packing her fur-trimmed fedora.

Upon arriving home that evening, she couldn't contain her excitement as she related her itinerary to Evelyn. Her friend expressed elation for her to have a getaway and made suggestions about which restaurants they should go to, even though she hadn't visited the city in thirty years. Mabel absorbed her ideas, not having gone since her childhood, but Evelyn's last tip didn't fly so well with her.

"Do you plan to go to Roy's on the way there or back?"

The notion didn't occur to her the whole day. "I don't intend to stop there at all."

"Why not? I wouldn't imagine you'd have to go far

off your route."

She shrugged. "Well, I'm not doing the driving, so I don't have much of a say in where the car goes."

"The Mabel Jennings I know has a say no matter what."

"Not when Audrey Detwiler is involved. Speaking of her, she's liable to steal him from me if I gave her the opportunity. That's how she ended up with two of her boyfriends, one of whom she married."

She chuckled and shook her head. "Roy wouldn't let that happen."

Mabel didn't counter the statement and dropped the matter. Evelyn complied for the time being, but she expected it to arise again before the week ended. She swallowed a hint of anger about the suggestion as the outing changed from a gift to a burden. Shame crept into her because she didn't consider the idea from the moment Frances invited her. Her guilt worsened when she realized she didn't want to arrange it, either. Did she love him as much as she'd grown to believe?

Falling back into her self-analysis, she attributed her reluctance to the fact that she wanted this trip to relieve her uncertainties about her future with Roy. How would it liberate her if she included him in it? She could just picture how it'd usher in further conflict and make her return home wishing she didn't bother to go at all.

She did her best to overcome her gloom and regain her optimism for the weekend trip, but she opted against informing Roy of it. She feared he'd follow the same logic Evelyn did. With how he liked to mention her visiting, he wouldn't overlook the occasion. Her agenda became more difficult to hide with every passing day. She'd have to admit her absence sooner or later, considering he'd call for their nightly chats. She just needed to decide if she should give him the true explanation for it.

"I could tell him I'm coming down with a cold and won't be able to talk for a few days," she strategized aloud to Evelyn over dinner Thursday. "I could write a couple letters for you to send out for me."

Evelyn scowled. "No, I'm not participating in lying to a good man. If you want to, it's your sin to make."

"I don't want to hurt him."

"Then surprise him on his doorstep."

Mabel wouldn't justify her reluctance to do so again. "I guess I could call him from the hotel. It costs a lot, but it's worth it if I can forego an argument."

"Don't you remember when you tried to disguise your identity from him? He didn't know you except for your voice, and he could still see through your dishonesty. He's too sharp to buy your mediocre acting skills."

She agreed with Evelyn's prediction and released a sigh. "The night before I met Roy, you told me love doesn't entail a bunch of fussing when it's real. If that's the case, I'm not sure what we have is the real deal. Things never seem to just fall into place."

"They did until you started standing in the way," Evelyn retorted.

She sat stone-faced, her nerves frayed from trying to fulfill her wishes and still appease Evelyn, Roy, and her own conscience. She lost her appetite and took her plate to the sink to clean it before she trotted upstairs to finish her packing in silence. Her suitcase lay open on the cedar chest at the end of her bed, and she took stock of what she already stuffed into it. She grabbed the last-minute necessities and realized she just needed a gown to wear to the theater. She put her hands on her hips, facing the same predicament she did when Roy took her out. She resisted picking the dress she wore then, but she drew it out due to her lack of a better option.

The clutch she carried complemented it so well that she wanted to take it, but she questioned whether or not she should. Because it contained her keepsakes from Roy, she deemed it unloving to strip it of such honor. She wouldn't empty Clark's things out of her box to accommodate anything short of the crown jewels. On the other hand, this would be temporary, and she could return everything to its place by Tuesday.

With a sigh, she removed the stack of letters and the souvenirs she archived from their dates. The heap it piled on her desk surprised her, considering she amassed it in so brief a period. The sight drudged up her regret for not giving him back the devotion he measured out to her. Adding to her remorse, she dipped into the inner pocket of the bag to take out the first piece of her collection, the engagement ring. Like the day she slipped it inside, she couldn't neglect marveling at its beauty and the precious sentiment it conveyed about its giver.

Interrupting her reverie, Evelyn hollered that Roy was on the phone. Dread permeating her stomach, she dropped the ring back into her purse, distracted, and marched down the stairs. All the way, she attempted to gather her thoughts to strike the right tone with Roy. She endeavored not to let on to her guilt, since she shouldn't have to apologize for living a life of her own. At the same time, she would display consideration for whatever feelings he expressed.

Evelyn's grimace when she handed off the receiver didn't help Mabel's attitude, but she suppressed her bitterness. Roy spoke in a cheery tone, so she decided to play along with the ordinary exchange and listen to his stories about work. She shared a couple from her day and debated pretending Frances popped in to invite her on the trip just that morning. As she strategized, she remembered Evelyn's earlier comment on her poor acting and decided against it.

Roy dragged the truth out of her with what should've been his closing words. "Well, honey, I'd better let you go before I sack out mid-sentence. I'm looking forward to having more energy to talk this weekend. I read there's a new special airing on Sunday."

"I'm sorry to say you'll have to watch it without me. As a matter of fact, I won't be home till Monday evening. A few girls I graduated with planned a little vacation and asked me to join them."

"That's great. Where are you ladies headed?"

She would've liked to get off without having to disclose their destination, but his optimism encouraged her to oblige him. "New York City. My girlfriend is a stage actress, and she wanted to give us a tour. She says she can get us tickets to see one of the major productions."

"How marvelous. I don't blame you for skipping out on me."

She exhaled, relieved he didn't take the smallest bit of offense. She resisted the urge to send a gloating smile Evelyn's way.

His next words put the brakes on her celebration.

"It must be a twelve-hour journey from there. Do you plan to stop anywhere?"

Her suppressed grin dimmed. "No. We don't have long to stay, so we want to pack in as much as we can."

"I understand. You should know Coatesville is right off the interstate. You wouldn't add an extra fifteen minutes to your trip by dropping by here. I'd love to take you all out for dinner."

Her chest tightened. "I appreciate it, but I can't commit to anything like that, being just a passenger. Believe me when I tell you our driver has a strong mind, and chances are she already has our route plotted out. She won't take suggestions or requests from any of us, least of all me."

"Sounds like the makings of an interesting few days." He chuckled, but she could perceive a change in his demeanor. "Would you consider taking a bus home and staying a night here? I could pay for your hotel room. You might need a break by then."

"That's sweet of you, but I can't. We're going to another show on Sunday, so we have to drive the whole way back on Monday." She hoped he'd remain reasonable.

He paused before making his next offer. "I don't have any big plans. Do you suppose I could swing over for a day and meet up with you?"

"I'm sorry, but again, I don't think I should agree to that without running it by my friends."

"I see." He accepted defeat, but even without making any blows, he didn't spare her from a battle wound to the heart. "I had to try. I never expected to find love again, and now that I have, I hate to squander any opportunity to see you. But I guess everyone has different priorities. Give me a call when you make it home."

The line went dead.

****

After the abrupt conclusion to the conversation, Mabel stole a peek at Evelyn and found her departing the room in silence. She deemed the separation a good thing, as she didn't care to relate the details of her exchange. In all truth, she probably didn't need to, with the dejected way she hung up telling the story.

During the hours that followed, her guilt stabbed her. She debated if she should withdraw from going on the controversial trip. At this point, her excitement for it vanished, and she doubted she could enjoy her time there because of the trouble it caused her. She couldn't help but wonder if the money she'd spend would prove to be a waste. Then again, she doubted canceling it would help matters, as it wouldn't remedy the issue that bothered Roy. If anything, it could project that she'd rather stay as far away from him as possible, even at the expense of a fun weekend.

Concluding her reasons to go outweighed the ones to bow out, she continued with her preparations, but the pain in Roy's sweet voice echoed through her. A glance at one of her photos of Clark reminded her this wasn't the first time her stubborn streak made her rebuff the man she loved.

****

For two months, Mabel and Clark wrote each other every day. Receiving his letters gave her the boost she needed to trudge through her many obligations. In her frequent moments of stress, the prospect of reading his words soothed her anxieties. She deemed most of her replies insufficient, a few sentences strung together usually around midnight. Even so, he always referred to them with high esteem.

On one of her rare Fridays off work, she devoted extra concentration to her response to his note from the previous day. He never asked for any favors besides his request to write, showing the utmost consideration for her busy life. For once, he made an appeal to her, albeit with the disclosure that he understood if she had to refuse. His graciousness made it harder to decline, especially since she so wanted to agree to it.

Her mom entered the room, her cane and slow pace still difficult to watch. Mabel rose to help her into her chair, but she waved her off.

"Are you writing to Clark?"

"Yep," Mabel stated with little expression.

"Don't bother to contain your excitement on my account."

"I'm not. I'm trying to figure out the best way to let him down."

"Let him down about what?"

Mabel didn't like to call attention to the sacrifices she made, but this time, she couldn't overlook it. "He wants me to be his date at his brother's wedding. He isn't looking forward to it because of how his dad and brother treat him, and he says I'd make it easier for him to face it. Obviously, I can't get away."

"And why not?"

She couldn't believe her mother would ask the question, but Mabel remained even-tempered. "Since Millie's working through the nights, I have to stick close by for you. Plus the telephone company won't give me any vacation time."

To Mabel's surprise, her sensitive mom didn't take exception to her tone but kept a sensible outlook, like she used to. "You can switch out your next day off with another girl. I can have your Aunt Lizzie help out for a weekend. She's offered to several times, and I think we should take her up on it."

For a moment, she warmed to the idea she might be able to join Clark, but it didn't take long to discover the snags.

"I don't have a way to get there."

"Could you ask Clark to drive down here to get you? We can pay him for gas."

He alluded to the possibility in his note, but she hated to trouble him like that again. "I'm sure he has a lot to do to help out his family."

"Brothers of the groom don't play much of a demanding role, but you decide what's best for you both."

She nodded, thanking her, and returned to her letter. She pondered her mother's suggestion and flipped to a new page to restart it. After a pause, she continued penning her regrets. As much as she yearned to be with Clark, she couldn't make another trip to Chicago. The city held nothing but dashed dreams and despair.

****

The past and present plagued Mabel for the entire night, crowding out any desire to sleep. When morning approached, she considered calling Roy again to apologize, but she feared it wouldn't help matters. Though contrite, she didn't want to change her plans, and he would sense that.

Before heading downstairs, she took account of

everything she needed to pack, zipping her suitcase once she satisfied her mental checklist. She lugged it down the staircase and propped it up by the door before she wandered into the kitchen for a quick bite. Truth be told, she didn't want to eat, but she figured she shouldn't head out on an empty stomach.

She greeted Evelyn but received no reply. While they ate breakfast, Duke made the lone sound between them with his snoring. Mabel polished off her toast quickly so she could escape the tense air, and she strolled into the living room to keep a lookout for Frances. The instant she spotted a teal car, she scurried to her suitcase and grabbed the doorknob. With her conscience pricking her, she announced her departure to Evelyn, who grumbled a farewell.

Mabel stepped outside, and Frances darted out of the sedan, wrapping her arms around her.

"This is going to be a blast!" She squeezed her tight. "I'm so happy you're coming with us."

Helen followed, but always having favored Audrey, she didn't manifest genuine cheer over the reunion. Mabel kept a smile glued to her face, even when her teenage rival approached her.

"Been a long time, Mabel. I couldn't believe how little you strayed from your childhood home."

Mabel bristled at the superior intonation of her voice. "I made a few rounds before I returned."

She beamed. "Yes, I heard about your stint in the hen house."

Frances played interference, taking her bag from her and passing it to Audrey. "Could you load this into the trunk?"

She complied while Frances babbled on about

getting tickets for a hit musical from one of her friends who performed in it. Her manner struck Mabel as strange, with her speech faster than usual. She seemed nervous, but Mabel couldn't determine the reason until she peeked inside the car and discovered it didn't have a back seat.

"Am I supposed to walk alongside you? I'm not sure my rear will fit beside the three of yours."

Audrey circled back over to them. "You'll have to forgive me, but I didn't expect you to join us. My husband removed the back bench years ago to give me room for all my shopping bags, but don't worry." She stuck her head into the car and hoisted out a stack of newspapers. "You'll have the comfiest ride of any of us."

Mabel's eyes narrowed in rage. "You expect me to sit on those clear from here to New York?"

Audrey had the audacity to take a gander at her behind. "I'd say you have enough padding to make do."

"Don't bother…" Her temper flaring, she lunged for the papers, but Frances stopped her and led her several yards away from the other two.

"I realize this isn't ideal, but we can work through it."

"Who's the *we* here? Your tush won't be squatted on a trash pile for twelve hours!"

"I'm willing to switch places with you if you'd rather."

She would've taken her up on it without a bit of guilt, but then she'd have to sit beside Audrey and Helen. "No, you don't have to."

Frances returned to the car and collected a blanket from under her seat. "I packed this along to give you extra cushioning, and my offer stands to trade with you anytime."

Her appeals didn't win over Mabel. "Look, I've had a rough week, and I don't need to be treated like a fifth wheel. Audrey's making it clear she doesn't want me around, so I'll let you guys go on your own."

"Please, don't do that. Don't give her that control over you. I want you with us, and if you back out, I'll book a flight home instead." She grasped her hand. "You've endured so much adversity in your life, and I've wanted to give you something special for a long time. Allow me to do that now."

She almost pointed out that Audrey was another form of adversity, but Frances's sincerity touched her. "Fine, but I need you to jog my memory."

"About what?"

"Audrey. Was she born in the elephants' train car or the apes'?"

Frances giggled, putting her arm around Mabel's shoulder.

****

Frances's words may have sent her into the car without argument, but their heartwarming effect didn't allay Mabel's anger for much longer than the time it took to get out of Louisville. Audrey used minimal caution when she drove over bumps, jolting Mabel's head into the roof. After a few not-so-accidental thumps, she stretched out to seize more legroom and didn't worry about kicking the bench once or twice—by mistake, of course.

When they crossed the Ohio border, she decided to quit seething and find a more comfortable position. The newspapers didn't offer value besides the amusement they gave Audrey, so she crouched down on the floor and put Frances's blanket underneath her. Between that and the carpet, she settled into a tolerable position, at least for a while.

Her physical aches waned the minute they entered Pennsylvania, as her emotional woes crowded them out with each Philadelphia sign she spotted. Roy once informed her Coatesville lay an hour west of the city, so she realized they'd passed through it when they entered the metro area. Her spirits dropped low, and the awful traffic jam they encountered did nothing to boost them. She recalled Roy's remark about not liking to drive there, and she started to long for the small town she'd been so determined to avoid.

Once they closed in on New York, her agony faded, and the anticipation that filled her earlier in the week returned. In an effort to claim a more optimal vantage point than the floor afforded, she mounted the newspapers for the remainder of the journey. From a distance, the city's skyline, which she marveled at in pictures, popped up and dwarfed everything around it. Enhancing its appearance, the orange sunset hung above Manhattan, with the lights switching on all around the town as dusk arrived.

With her hips throbbing, Mabel cheered inside when they rode through the Lincoln Tunnel. Frances told them her Fourteenth Street apartment wasn't far from it, and within minutes, she instructed Audrey to park at her building's curb.

Audrey took the keys out of the ignition and shifted toward Frances. "Will your valet park the car?"

"No, we don't have a garage here, which is why I don't drive. Your hotel has one."

Her eyes grew large. "Hotel? Aren't we staying with you?"

"Didn't I tell you I only have two bedrooms? Mabel will take my spare one, and I'm paying for a room for you guys. It's on Twenty-Third." She opened the door. "Follow me, Mabel. I'm so stiff and can't imagine how cramped you must be. We should go for a dip in the pool before it closes for the night."

It took all of Mabel's restraint not to crack up as she pried her body out of the back and noted the stunned expression on Audrey's face. "You ladies enjoy your evening."

Frances lifted both of their bags from the trunk and passed off Mabel's, going up to the passenger's window to give Audrey directions to the hotel. After watching them drive away, she and Mabel broke into hysterical laughter.

"When did you decide to do that?" Mabel asked.

"I made the reservations from the first rest stop. I knew it would make Audrey squirm since she kept asking me about my place all week long. She deserves it in light of what she pulled on you. I promised you I'd make this special."

She hugged her with one arm. "I couldn't have dreamed of anything better."

A doorman greeted them, addressing Frances by name and asking if she enjoyed her trip. After she answered in the affirmative, she introduced him as Arthur to Mabel and informed him Mabel would be staying there for the weekend. He wished them a nice visit and granted them entry into the lobby, which wowed Mabel. Countless chandeliers hung from the high ceiling, their lights ricocheting off the white leather-covered furniture. Accented by marble columns scattered throughout the expanse, it clearly catered to the wealthy. She gaped at the contrast between it and the small cottage where Frances grew up.

Frances led her to the elevator and engaged with its attendant much like she did the doorman. Observing her friend in action tickled Mabel, but she didn't envy the lifestyle. She found it exhausting to have to interact like that with somebody all the time. They stepped out on the twenty-eighth floor and made their way to Frances's apartment. More ogle-worthy features surrounded the place, with gold sconces and an array of paintings on the walls. To top it off, seven-foot-tall windows offered incredible views of the city below.

She set down her suitcase by the door and strolled over to one of them to take in the scenery. She couldn't dispute the beauty of lush forests and open landscapes, but in her estimation, nothing could beat the twinkling glamor of a city.

"This"—Mabel spread out her arms at the setting—"makes up for the tortuous ride."

Frances joined her in her gazing. "This sold the place to me. I spent twenty years fantasizing about having more to look at than other people's windows or parking lots. I couldn't miss my chance at it once my finances allowed it."

Mabel wished she could've seized her dreams like that. "I love Louisville, but when I met Clark in Chicago, everything I saw there drew me. The night of Mom and Dad's accident, I hinted to Clark that I'd consider moving there if I ever had a good enough reason to. He winked at me, saying he might be able to think of one. The moment passed so quickly, but it took me so long to accept it couldn't happen."

"But your love didn't suffer because of your location."

She shrugged. "Living with Mom and Millie didn't make for the ideal environment for newlyweds."

"What if he'd waited for your circumstances to permit you to return and have that future in Chicago, instead of leaving his world behind to help you carry your load? Would it have meant as much to you?"

Mabel stared down at the mahogany floor, considering the scenario. Given her mom lived for years after Clark's death, they couldn't have reunited if he didn't take the initiative. Plus his willingness to marry her in spite of her challenges proved his deep love for her. "No."

Frances pivoted to face her. "I may have told you Monday that I never married because of wanting my freedom, but that isn't altogether true. I would've if I'd found someone like that. A man who loved me enough to want to take my side when the bottom dropped out from underneath me. Most of the guys around here won't even try to catch your fall for fear of breaking a nail. They don't give a hoot if you missed out on a part, so long as they landed one."

Mabel appreciated her honesty. The remark reminded her of Roy's words to her days before, when he expressed his desire to make her happy. Frances's words showed her how much she should've cherished such loving care rather than be agitated by it.

Dropping the serious talk, Mabel asked her for a tour of the rest of her apartment. Her friend agreed without hesitation, but she warned her that her housekeeper hadn't worked there for a month. None of the rooms implied a lack of attention, aside from a couple of dusty surfaces and a few clean dishes beside the sink Frances didn't put away before her trip. As she admired the spacious place, Mabel continued to grin over how Frances forced Audrey and Helen into a hotel. While she told the truth about having two bedrooms, the large beds could've held three people each, and someone could've used her long couch in a pinch. Anybody could tell she could've accommodated them if she wanted to, flattering Mabel that much more.

They made their last stop in the guest bedroom, which she guessed measured the same size as her and Evelyn's whole first story. Frances pointed out the phone on the vanity and assured her she could use it any time.

"I'll give you some privacy to call your Pennsylvania sweetheart. Try to keep it under four hours." She winked.

"Thanks, but I'm not planning to check in with him until I get back home."

"Merry Time Mabel never did need a fellow to have fun, did she?"

"No, ma'am. But I'd better tell Evelyn we arrived safely."

She nodded and doubled down on her invitation to go for a quick swim, reporting the pool would close in forty-five minutes. Once alone, Mabel meandered to the phone and dialed with a sigh, doubtful she'd receive an amiable response from her disapproving friend. Evelyn proved her right, uttering a mere six words in the entire exchange.

She resisted the temptation to let her sourness fester and brushed off the cold treatment. Thankful she packed her bathing suit on a whim, she put it on along with her robe and met Frances by the front door to head to the pool. They found it crowded and couldn't spot a big enough space that would allow them to stretch out at first. Once the closing time approached, the tenants filtered out and gave them a chance to take a dip, at least to loosen up their sore muscles.

They shared a bowl of potato chips after they returned to the apartment, but they didn't linger for long into the night like they used to as kids at slumber parties. Mabel glided between the soft sheets on her bed and expected to fall right to sleep due to her tiring day. She didn't find it so easy, soon discovering a caveat to the city's glitzy lights—nobody ever switched them off. The sheer curtains hanging in the window didn't function as anything but decoration, which failed to shield her eyes from the relentless glow outside. Recalling the heavy velvet ones in Frances's room, she surmised she hadn't made a mistake when choosing decor for her guests. She must've wanted to insure they kept their visits short.

Mabel flipped over, away from the window, and tried to relax. Still, her mind wouldn't cooperate, instead recapping her trip to that point. Her emotional struggles stood out from the rest of her misadventures, in particular her conversation with Frances about Clark. Her thoughts drifted back to the day Frances referred to, when he sacrificed everything for her.

****

After Mabel sent her regrets, Clark extended multiple assurances that he understood why she couldn't attend his brother's wedding. Nonetheless, she sensed a change in him in the following weeks. His letters became less frequent and shorter, and they didn't express the tender feelings they used to. Mabel feared she hurt him and that it might've led him to reconsider their relationship. The supposition broke her heart, but she concluded it may be for the best. She couldn't give him her all like most young women without responsibilities could. If he couldn't accept that, she didn't blame him. He displayed such immense compassion from the moment they met, and she owed it to him to let him go if he desired.

She started to believe she'd have to make that choice when the week after the wedding passed without a word from him. Remorse hit her unlike ever before, as it sank in how unfairly she treated him. He supported her and her family more in a few days than a lot of men would in a lifetime, but she couldn't take his side when he needed her.

She pondered what she should say in her next letter and whether or not it should be her last. Wracking her brain, she sat at the kitchen table with a paper and pen, but a knock on the door halted her deliberation.

She peeked out at the front porch and recognized the familiar figure. In some ways, his touch still lingered on her skin from when they embraced on the porch. Another part of her, however, worried she imagined him altogether because of how distant the memory of him ebbed from her grasp.

She opened the door. "Clark?"

He smiled, appearing delighted by her bewilderment. "Hi, Mabel."

The tenderness in his voice sent a mix of joy and agony through her, but she masked it with wit. "What brings you to this side of the Ohio River?"

"*I wanted to tell you about the wedding, but I would've developed writer's cramp if I'd penned it.*"

She cocked her head, playful. "*And you found it preferable to drive for six hours?*"

He took her hand. "*My destination gave me the incentive I needed.*"

She stepped over the threshold and shut the door behind her. She anticipated a kiss from him, but he didn't lean in for one. He sat down in the same spot where he cradled her moments before he journeyed home. She worried he chose the setting to make his final goodbye, but his firm grip kindled hope in her.

A pit of guilt formed in her stomach. "*I'm assuming it lived up to your expectations?*"

"*No, it surpassed them but in a good way. My dad showed me more respect than he ever has, and my brother's wife claimed he's spoken well of me. We posed for what I think is our first family picture, so I'd call it a success.*"

She wondered why he'd have difficulty writing the three-sentence description, but she chose not to ask. "*I'm glad to hear that.*"

He shrugged. "*I bet you enjoy hearing it as much as I enjoyed experiencing it, if not more. Don't get me wrong, I liked not being forced to question my existence by the end of the night, but I didn't leave with much fulfillment, either. I've wished for so long he'd dignify me with a pat on the back and a word or two of praise at best. When he gave it to me, nothing changed. I'm still no more than the disappointment of a son. I guess that could be my own thinking, but he hasn't done a great deal to convince me otherwise.*"

She put her head on his shoulder. "*Making amends*

takes a long time after years of mistreatment. Maybe you'll be able to start anew from this point forward."

"I suppose." His words didn't brim with confidence. He leaned his body farther away from her, making her worry she upset him. "All the while I was with him, I kept remembering your dad and the way he interacted with you and Millie, even me. He made it clear he didn't trust me, but he never gave me the idea he didn't like me, as my father does."

"He did like you, and like I told you before, he had more trouble trusting me than he did you."

He chuckled. "Regardless, his world revolved around you guys, and in my opinion, that's what has held you all together in his absence. You attest to it in everything you're doing, and I'm awestruck by it. I have no idea how my family would handle a situation like this, but I'm sure we couldn't compare to you."

She bit her lip, in an attempt not to cry. "You wouldn't be so inspired if you saw me every day."

"I'm willing to take that risk." He took out a ring from his pocket. "I love my family, and I'll miss my mom, but I need to be in yours. I need you."

****

His words warmed her heart, even as she lay in bed years later. She agreed with her whole heart that nothing marred their love, including where they lived, as Frances said. The hardships they faced together served to draw them closer and may have given them a better life than the one they might've led in Chicago. Every time he helped her mom to walk or offered her or Millie a sympathetic ear, her love for him grew. Marrying her didn't present him with the easy route, but he always made it clear he didn't want to take any other one.

In her ruminating, she realized the converse side, that Irvington didn't doom her and Ned to unhappiness. Sure, the lifestyle added to their friction now and then, but they could've weathered those differences if they shared a stronger love. Clark proved love didn't depend on convenience, timing, or location.

So how could she hold those counts against Roy?

Chapter Nine

To her surprise, Mabel slept for a solid eight hours and didn't wake until nine. Having been an early riser by nature, some shame washed over her. She hated to lose out on time with Frances and didn't want to delay any of her plans for them. She rushed to get dressed and put some powder on her cheeks. When she emerged from the bedroom, she found out she didn't need to hurry, given Frances had yet to stir. Her slow start made sense, considering their long trip as well as her routine of staying up late for her performances every night.

Figuring they'd both need a boost, she put on a pot of coffee, a novelty for her now that she and Evelyn switched to instant. She downed half a cup before Frances rounded the hallway.

"You didn't have to make that bitter stuff. I have something else for you to try at breakfast. It beats your typical cup of joe by a mile. I haven't made coffee in months."

Many of her coworkers adopted the same habit of buying their caffeine fix. She deemed it a waste, but she wouldn't admit it to Frances. "Be assured I'll take as much help as I can get to stay awake. I couldn't adjust to sleeping with the city lights glaring in the room. I debated if I should put on suntan lotion."

Frances nodded. "I didn't get accustomed to it for years, either."

"Yeah, until you bought some actual curtains for your room and gave your guests the fancy worthless ones. You don't want much company, do you?"

Other women may have taken offense at her blunt manner, but Frances offered a coy grin. "You've met my family."

They shared a laugh, and Frances promised to make up for her restless night. She called Audrey and Helen's hotel room to tell them they could pick them up and that she'd direct them to the restaurant where they'd have breakfast. Mabel continued to relish the way she treated Audrey like a servant. More than that, the women's dissatisfied expressions when they stopped at the curb delighted her. Audrey lauded the hotel when she greeted Frances, but she didn't manifest the superior air she displayed the previous day. Her demotion from her uppity podium made the newspaper stack softer to Mabel as they traveled through town.

Philadelphia's traffic didn't compare to the jam they ran into in Manhattan. Once they navigated out of a backup near Frances's building, the congestion lessened but far exceeded the busiest day in Louisville. Frances dictated the best route to Greenwich Village, where they pulled up to a café. As they strolled inside, she related the history of her favorite breakfast eatery, which boasted that it introduced the cappuccino to America.

To oblige Frances, Mabel ordered the beverage and watched it being made by the original Italian-made machine, which announced its old age with its clunky noises. Despite her love of sweets, Mabel found it too sugary when paired with her pancakes. She didn't vocalize her opinion, not wanting to disappoint her.

Regardless, she enjoyed the chance to not have to cook or clean up for a change.

She followed Francis's lead for the rest of the day, as they explored the city. While in Greenwich Village, Frances guided them to the boutique she mentioned when she first invited her on the trip, and Mabel understood why she gave it such high praise. She never browsed such a unique collection of accessories and clothing, and the prices were lower than she predicted. They each carried out a couple of bags full of goodies, with Mabel finding a necklace to wear to the play that evening.

Afterward, they took a ride on the ferry to Ellis Island and then trekked across town to traverse Central Park. Before they returned downtown, they squeezed in a bit more shopping on Fifth Avenue, which pandered to a wealthier clientele than the boutique. Mabel couldn't afford anymore than a bottle of perfume for Evelyn, but the others bought so much that it left her surrounded by packages on the drive back.

They grabbed takeout from a Chinese restaurant and took it to Frances's place. Mabel sensed her hesitance to invite Audrey and Helen, in all likelihood because of the comfortable lodging she denied them. Obligated, she offered they could pick up their dresses and change there after they ate dinner together. Mabel would've liked some separation from them, but she couldn't wait to observe Audrey's reaction to the noticeable slighting.

Determined not to give away her fascination, she fixed her eyes in the opposite direction of them during their jaunt up to the apartment. She weaseled her way in front of the two when Frances unlocked her door. She stole a sly glance at her nemeses as she hung her purse on the coat rack. She gleaned great pleasure from noting Audrey's face undergo several transformations. Her initial admiration evolved into disturbance and irritation, until it made its final descent to contempt.

She sneered. "Well, isn't this cozy?"

Mabel spun around to conceal her jubilation.

Frances remained nonchalant. "It's simple, compared to the penthouses some of my friends have, but I like it. After spending all day under the stage lights, I crave a relaxed environment."

"That's why she has those thick velvet drapes." Mabel winked at her, not elaborating on their joke from that morning.

Audrey stayed quiet throughout most of their meal, and while she enjoyed seeing her sulk, Mabel grew tired of the spoiled child act. Frances paid for everything they did together, giving none of them the right to complain. To her relief, Audrey snapped out of her hissy fit as their night at the theater drew close. Nonetheless, her scorn for Mabel intensified to the point where she wouldn't face her. Her hostility didn't taint Mabel's evening, since she learned long ago not to rely on her to contribute anything good to her life.

With three hours to go before show time, the women dispersed to primp themselves. Like she predicted, Audrey and Helen reverted to their juvenile ways of being codependent in every move they made. They did each other's hair and makeup and bantered about countless concerns. Sitting at the vanity in her room, Mabel rolled her eyes again and again over the commotion they created in the adjacent bathroom. She never fussed to such a degree, even for special occasions. Rather, she stuck to her usual face regimen and put a few more curlers in her hair than usual. She finished up before either of them decided on an eyeshadow color.

Her focus shifted when she put on her dress, her reflection the same as it had been two months ago on the night of her date with Roy. The feel of the fabric reminded her of his touch, and she caught whiffs of his cologne on the scarf where he put his arm around her shoulder. She'd always think of it as the dress she wore for him, but she wondered if he'd remember it with similar fondness. She could tell he loved her in it when he first gazed at her, but would her rejection of him now mask its beauty?

She dismissed the thought so she wouldn't revert to her wallowing, rationalizing that, as a man, he probably wouldn't have any memory of what she donned. Returning to the present, she dug her clutch out of her luggage and waltzed out to the hallway to swap her wallet from her pocketbook into it. Frances cut her off halfway there, needing someone to give her a hand with her zipper.

Mabel mused at her emerald green satin gown, which had a halter top and a short train. "This is stunning."

"Thank you. I wore it to an opening night a couple of years back. People disapprove of it when an actress reuses an outfit, but I can't resist with this one."

"I can't fathom how you handle the critics like you do."

"Mom prepared me well." She smiled, glancing in the mirror. "Are those two ready yet?"

"I doubt it. Helen still hasn't figured out where

lipstick goes."

She shook her head, but a glint in her eye revealed the humor she found in the quip. Mabel followed her to the bathroom door, which she tapped as she announced they'd arrive late if they dallied much longer. Sounding like teenagers, the two pledged to finish *in a second.* Mabel and Frances rolled their eyes and sat down in anticipation of a lengthy wait.

Upon realizing she forgot to put her wallet into her bag, Mabel crossed the room to retrieve it. After she dropped it inside, she spotted the sparkle of the ring Roy gave her. Alarmed, she retraced her actions at home, when she meant to secure it elsewhere, and she soon stumbled on the moment when things went awry. She'd paused to study the gem, but Roy's call distracted her from proceeding to tuck it away. Instead, she placed it back where it now lay without a second thought.

She plucked it out to take it into her bedroom and stash it in her suitcase. Before she could, Audrey and Helen sashayed through the hall, declaring they were all set. Frances rushed over and herded them toward the door so they wouldn't take on any further alterations.

Mabel couldn't argue with her, so she released the ring back into the bottom of the purse with the resolve to keep it close to her.

****

From their seats in the lower balcony, the four ladies stood up with the rest of the crowd to give the cast an ovation. The audience tossed dozens of bouquets onto the stage as the actors took a final bow, and the curtain closed. Sweating from the exhilaration of it and the stuffy auditorium, Mabel couldn't imagine how the performers withstood heat exhaustion.

The play entertained her, with the songs catchy and the portrayals hilarious. That said, she struggled not to get absorbed in the plot's love story. She attached many of her and Roy's experiences to those of the lead characters. The man, a bachelor, didn't manifest Roy's kindness, but his motivations for wanting a wife—to tend to the house for him—raised her suspicions of him. At the same time, his later confessions of having a dull life without his love interest touched her, reminding her of Roy's similar confessions. By the closing scene, she fell back into her state of unrest.

Frances's colleague fulfilled her promise to get them passes to meet the cast afterward, but she advised them not to show up at the designated corridor for fifteen minutes. The request didn't prove difficult, taking into account the crush of the departing crowd. Mabel lost track of the others while in the stairway but eyeballed them ahead before long.

She welcomed the slow pace, which permitted her extra time to absorb the spectacular surroundings. The theater's beauty captivated her the whole night. More than once, she strained to concentrate her attention on the performance because of the ornate furnishings around her. With a plethora of gold accents, the regal design showcased its European influences, from the wreaths of leaves painted on the ceiling, to the cast-iron gallery on the building's façade. As she peered out at it from the landing of the staircase, she basked in the magnificence.

When they navigated to the passage that led backstage, enough time had elapsed to grant them immediate access. Frances navigated to the front of them, and Audrey leapt to her side to get autographs as

Frances conversed with the stars. Another group of guests trailed behind them, so she didn't chat long with anyone besides the chorus singer who gave her the tickets. Mabel appreciated the privilege of the personal experience, but she didn't mind not being able to get too chummy, recognizing they were just people with a prestigious career.

After they weaved through the line, they followed the signs to the lobby to exit. Mabel soaked in the enchanting views the whole way. She didn't notice Frances halt her steps to wait for her until she locked arms with her.

"Breathtaking, isn't it?" Frances remarked.

"Absolutely. Have you performed here?"

"No. They don't book anything but the major hits. Every actor in town dreams of working here, for more reasons than the glorious setting. I used to think I'd get my chance, but I'm afraid it would've happened by now if it was ever going to."

Mabel winked at her. "Don't give up on it. We don't have a foot in the grave yet."

They giggled, opening the double doors ahead. Audrey and Helen advanced quite far on the way to the garage where they parked, not indicating any desire to join them. Mabel considered it distasteful, but she embraced the space and time alone with her friend.

The warm breeze caressed her face, adding to the city's splendor. She perused the sights around her, not wanting to miss anything. As she craned her neck to catch a glimpse of nearby Times Square, a man called Frances's name. Mabel didn't pay it much notice until Frances stopped and took a piece of paper from him.

"My wife's a big fan, Ms. Baxter. She begs me to

take her every time she hears you're starring in a show."

Frances scribbled her signature. "Tell her I'll be appearing in a new production that opens in October. I hope to see you both there."

Squinting to spot Audrey and Helen's figures, Mabel prepared to amble on to catch up with them, but the sight of a beggar standing a few feet away made her pause. He scowled at Frances and her fan, wearing his thoughts of the unjust contrast between his lot in life and hers. He was white, but she reflected on Roy's kindness to the Black fellow and followed his example by getting some money out of her purse to give him. She extended it to him, but instead of offering a word of appreciation, he grabbed her wrist and put a knife to her throat.

He spit a demand into her ear. "Give me everything you have!"

"Mabel!" Frances started toward her, but her supposed admirer seized her arm.

He pulled a gun out from behind him and aimed it at her. "The same goes for you, Starlet."

Mabel heeded the advice she'd heard before about such a dilemma, emptying all the cash from her wallet. Panic enveloped her when she noted the engagement ring, unprotected from detection if her attacker insisted on peeking inside. In an attempt to discourage that, she stuffed her money into his palm.

"Jewelry, too," he demanded.

With a firm grip on her clutch, she yanked off her necklace and clip-on earrings, even though they didn't offer any value. She didn't want to argue, in hopes of making it through this alive and with Roy's ring.

"That's everything I have."

He let go of her but kept ahold of his knife. Scrutinizing his expression, she couldn't discern if he would challenge her claim or not. Frances's cry made them both jerk their heads around. Mabel's chest tightened with terror when the other mugger shoved her friend to the ground.

Frances clutched her pearl necklace with her left hand and held up her right one in defense. "Please, sir, these belonged to my grandmother."

"All the more valuable." He bent down on one knee and batted away her arm. She didn't stop thrashing, so he disengaged the safety on his revolver. "Don't make me use this."

In hysterics, she didn't let up in her pleas. Mabel wanted to race to her aid and even give up her ring in exchange for the pearls, but the threat of the two men with their weapons paralyzed her. Apparently in a helpful mood, too, the purported beggar darted to his accomplice and bumped into Mabel, knocking her bag from her trembling hands. She didn't want to alert him to its worth, but she couldn't let it go. Bending down with discretion, her finger grazed it at the moment he glanced over his shoulder.

He lunged at it. "Allow me."

Just before he secured it in his grasp, a policeman blew his whistle from the opposite side of the street. Unfazed, he stretched down to capture it, but a squad car sped toward the curb and made him cower.

He dashed to his partner's side, but the man refused to give up until he broke off Frances's pearls. The stones spilled onto the pavement, where he recovered a couple of them. The majority remained scattered as they escaped in haste.

An officer barreled out of the vehicle. "Freeze!"

The felons defied the command, bolting the other way with their plunder.

****

Mabel and Frances sat close together in the police station, relating those horrific moments to a detective. Mabel couldn't believe how little she recalled from an unforgettable event that occurred less than an hour earlier. Scarce as her memory was, she gave him a more detailed description of her assailant than Frances could. She failed to remember his blond hair or rectangular glasses. Given the two's brief exchange before the confrontation, Mabel expected her to have a better recollection. As she listened, she concluded the star's frequent encounters with fans robbed her retention of them. Plus she figured the trauma her sensitive friend felt surpassed her distress, considering how he threw her to the ground.

They held hands during the interview, and the abrasions on Frances's neck pained Mabel. She surmised the mugger inflicted them during his forceful attempts to snatch her grandmother's pearls. Mabel wondered if the thieves would've relented easier if she'd surrendered her ring, but she doubted criminals compromised like that.

After they finished giving their statements, the detective dismissed them with the assurance that the department would do their utmost to find the men. Mabel didn't put much faith in it, considering he admitted the increase in muggings that summer. Frances also shared she'd suffered one in her first year of living there. Though she didn't say it, Mabel inferred

175

the authorities didn't detain the perpetrator then. With the surge in them now, she didn't foresee this resulting in a different outcome.

They met up with Audrey and Helen in the precinct's waiting area, and the streaks of mascara on their cheeks let on that they'd been crying. They'd sprinted down the sidewalk at the same time the police arrived, and both of them wore guilt on their faces. They exchanged hugs once the commotion subsided, and they opened their arms again when she and Frances rounded the corner. Mabel never would've believed Audrey would extend comfort to her, much less that she'd welcome it, but the gesture gave her a measure of peace.

Just the same, she yearned for Roy's comfort, and despite the horror of everything that happened, she couldn't think of anyone but him. Ever since the altercation, she envisioned the scenario of having him there. She believed to her core he would've kept them safe if the men had dared to accost them in the presence of his tall stature. More than that, he would've provided her serenity, as he did when they encountered the conflict at the Ferris wheel. She wished she'd allowed him to join them like he yearned to, both at the theater and at this very moment.

They wandered through the door of Frances's apartment a few minutes past two o'clock, too late to call either him or Evelyn. She didn't care to talk, anyhow, and Frances didn't seem to, either. Having hugged Audrey and Helen but not each other, they embraced for the first time all day. Frances sobbed into Mabel's shoulder, compelling her to weep.

After they regained composure, Frances drew

away. "You deserve a good night's rest. Why don't you sleep in my room? My bed's plenty big."

She nodded in agreement and whispered a thank-you. She perceived Frances wanted the security of having someone else close by more than anything, and she didn't fault her for it. She desired the same.

Going into her bedroom to change out of her clothes, she caught sight of her reflection, and her heart ached with anguish. The dress she cherished because of her memories of Roy now represented tragedy. Her beloved scarf called to mind the knife being held up to her, and her clutch bore invisible stains left by her frantic rummaging. Despite it all, she found her ring inside, glistening as brightly as ever. A tear trickled down her cheek as she reflected on how it symbolized resilience and hope, topped by Roy's love for her.

Slipping under the covers of Frances's massive bed, she contemplated whether or not her ability to safeguard the ring foreshadowed anything with regard to their future. Could they too be rescued from what appeared to be an unsolvable situation? She realized a lot of that depended on her. While the incident made her view matters with a different perspective, her independence combined with guilt restrained her from leaning on him the way she wanted to. She'd sound selfish and weak if she confessed to wishing he could've protected her. Plus she refused to crawl back to a man on such grounds. She didn't marry either of her husbands for physical or financial security, and she wouldn't start now.

Her analysis led her to the truth that she didn't pine for Roy as a mere bodyguard; she longed to experience the good and the bad with him. The entire trip, she pictured his reaction to various facets of it, for no other reason than the joy he added to her life. For years, she wouldn't let a man govern her happiness, based on her trials with one who never loved her in the first place. Roy—who left her with no uncertainty of his devotion—broke down that barrier, even beyond her willingness to allow him.

She couldn't figure out how to tell him that or if it would matter to him. She gave him the run-around from the first time they met, and he always accepted it with mercy and humor. With her latest stunt of avoiding him like this, she feared he might not show her such forgiveness.

She didn't have a clear plan to make amends with Roy, but for the moment, she set her mind on getting out of New York pronto. She yearned to carry out the rest of Francis's itinerary, but the mugging robbed her of the nerve and the money to stick around the city. She couldn't figure out how she'd get home on her own since she couldn't afford a bus ticket, but she wouldn't let anything deter her from fleeing town.

To her relief, Audrey announced the same goal when she and Helen arrived at the apartment the next morning for breakfast. Her husband demanded she return to Louisville without delay. Frances lowered her eyes and expressed her disappointment for them to go under the dire circumstances, but Mabel doubted her friend could've mustered the fortitude to entertain them. Still, a part of her hated to dash off, with Frances in such a vulnerable state.

Already having packed their bags, the two waited for Mabel to collect her effects. She buried her clutch with the ring deep under her clothes in case of a second misfortune. As she zipped it shut, a tap thumped on the open door, and Frances moseyed through it. She closed it behind her and approached Mabel, stretching out for another hug.

"I'm so sorry. I wanted this trip to lighten your load, not add to it." Her voice cracked.

"It didn't. It was nothing but a terrifying moment, and we both walked away from it. That's what counts And now, you don't have to worry about me moving in with you."

She laughed. "I thought the curtains already scared you off."

"I had ideas." After the levity passed, Mabel grasped her hand. "Are you going to be all right?"

She nodded. "I'll have to use more caution. I made the same resolve last time, but that paled in comparison to this. Back then, the jerk took my cash and ran. The world is changing, and I'm afraid a big part of that isn't for the better."

Mabel embraced her once more and thanked her for including her. Frances's words about the changing world resounded through Mabel's brain long after they departed. Little by little, she'd become aware of the prevalence of violence and unrest that crept into Louisville and many other cities, but she tried to shy away from the reality of it. Living in a busy town shaped her, and she railed against anything that shook her trust in it. Now she reconsidered her stance, reflecting again on Frances's statement that location didn't define one's happiness.

Questions about her long-term future stirred up in her thoughts once more. She realized her age and experience tricked her into the belief that she controlled her own fate. That's why she didn't want to forfeit her freedom by following Roy as she did Ned. She became convinced she could elude changes because of how many life had already thrown at her.

But the world didn't operate that way. It changed, and she supposed she should, too.

****

As they traveled through town, Mabel fixed her eyes on the small houses and woodlands they passed. She ogled at the grandeur of the bustling city forty-eight hours earlier, but the simplicity and homeness now appealed to her for the first time. Old brick buildings didn't rival the magnificence of New York's modern skyscrapers, and the downtown area could fit in one borough, but the scene gave her a sense of belonging.

Audrey stopped at the first gas station along their route and asked Mabel to pump it while she headed inside the store to pay. The three of them cooperated well for the duration of the drive, being side-by-side in the one seat. They engaged in occasional chitchat, but she wouldn't claim they developed a true bond. Audrey and Helen seemed sympathetic to the ordeal she endured, and they evidently decided to take a hiatus from their lifelong campaign against her. Nevertheless, she mustered a lot of courage to entreat them for their assistance to initiate her plan, and they astounded her when they agreed.

Audrey emerged from the store right as Mabel screwed the cap on the tank.

"The cashier gave me directions." She smiled and displayed a slip of paper. "He recognized the address as Roy's without me saying anything."

Small towns. She rolled her eyes but resisted giving

in to her deep-rooted stereotype. "Did he ask any questions?"

"He looked curious, so I told him we were dropping by from out-of-town and left it at that."

All in a single weekend, they hugged, sat for hours in the same car, and now conspired together. She wouldn't forget this so-called vacation.

She conveyed her appreciation. Before ducking back into the car, she asked Audrey to open the trunk so she could access her suitcase. She retrieved the outfit she hadn't worn yet, a red blouse with a ruffle on the front and a black skirt. She considered it rather plain, but she preferred it to the dress she sweated in all morning. She carried it to the restroom, despite her reluctance to change somewhere that never boasted ideal conditions. The tidy room surpassed her expectations.

In her fresh clothes, she evaluated her reflection in the mirror, anxiety gripping her. How would Roy react to her unexpected visit? Had his anger brewed in the days following their last conversation, embittering him against her? Would he even be home?

Her angst plagued her for the short journey until Audrey slowed her speed to turn into a driveway. Mabel spotted the number on the mailbox that confirmed it to be his, and the truck parked beside the shed cleared up her worries over his whereabouts. Her eyes focused on the simple two-story house, which matched what she anticipated of her love's home. Painted her favorite shade of blue, the property's quaintness reflected his unpretentious nature. At the same time, the delicate features, like the trellis on the porch and the crown molding over the windows, hinted to his romantic quality.

Audrey didn't drive the whole way up to the stone pathway, prepared to back out if Roy opened the door. Mabel agreed to meet them at a nearby park when she finished. She tiptoed out onto the ground, a bundle of nerves, and strode ahead. The well-manicured lawn distracted her from her trepidation. She chuckled as she recalled one of his letters in which he mentioned repairing his mower and complained about mechanical work.

On the steps, she took in a deep breath, and her eyes fell to the ring in her palm. She fought back her tears and punched the doorbell. Everything remained still for a second, but at last, the knob twisted.

Astonishment covered Roy's face, no doubt mirroring her expression when Clark appeared on her steps. "Mabel?"

On the other end this time, she grasped for the right words, wishing she could handle it with the same suaveness as Clark. During the drive, she decided not to bring up the mugging so he wouldn't get the idea that she ran to him out of fear, but she failed to formulate an alternative. In the end, she let her heart do the speaking.

"We cut our trip short, and I couldn't go home without talking to you in person. I've realized the unkind way I've treated you, not just on this occasion but ever since we met. I kept refusing to admit it, but I withheld my heart from loving someone again. When we first went out, I did it to prove my niece wrong because she charged me with that exact claim."

He smirked much like he did when he caught her trying to fool him on their first date. "I don't know whether to thank her or scold her for that."

"I've done both, trust me. I expected us to have a nice dinner at best and part our separate ways afterward. You seemed like a safe option because you'd leave town in a few days, so why not? But I underestimated you, and I didn't grasp that until it was too late, until you'd snuck past all my defenses. You captured my heart, even if I wanted to keep you out of it. That said, I don't surrender to any battle without a fight, and that's why I've done so much to sabotage our future together."

He put his hands into his pockets, his eyes solemn. "Yes, you have."

She swallowed hard and continued her confession. "Besides hurting you, I most regret boxing you into the confines of what I wanted you to mean to me. I resisted it when you moved me like Clark used to, but I bucked at it if you did anything that resembled Ned in the most remote way. You're neither of them, and I'm sorry it took me this long to accept that.

"You're Roy, a man who's witnessed my scatterbrained moments but still loves me and even trusts me to help him grow. I apologize for failing to reciprocate that to you. I'd like the opportunity to do better, but I understand if you don't want to give it to me." She extended her hand to him.

He took it without a word. As she hoped, he soon glanced downward, noticing the ring she slid on her finger right before he answered the door. Remaining silent, he pivoted away from her to pick up something behind him. He passed her a note. "I wrote this to send you tomorrow."

She caught her breath, her dreams fading away.

Epilogue

May 2005

Mabel peered around the banquet hall, observing her guests along with the photographs sprinkled through the room. She and Roy well made up for their lack of pictures during their first week together back in Louisville, amassing countless of them in their forty years of marriage. With her help, Bev selected the best ones from their travels to all fifty states mixed in with some from their everyday routine. Although their differences in choices of entertainment sometimes clashed, she persuaded him to venture out of Coatesville. Meanwhile, he opened her eyes to the simple pleasures their small town offered.

Bev approached her, wrapping her arm around her aunt. "Does it meet your satisfaction?"

"It goes far beyond that, sweetie. Thank you so much for your hard work."

She straightened her posture, grinning. "Well, as the person who's responsible for bringing you two together, I wanted to show off my achievement."

"Before you take all the credit, why don't you try putting up with your uncle for the next forty years?"

"I'd trade places with you, but I wouldn't switch with Uncle Roy!"

Mabel gave her hand a gentle swat, treasuring how

their companionship remained constant all this time. After Millie's husband retired, they moved to the area, and since Bev hadn't settled down yet, she joined them. Having lived away from them for twelve years by then, Mabel welcomed their arrival.

Bev led her to the gift table, where she and Roy's daughter-in-law, Rebecca, set up a special arrangement in tribute to the couple's love story. They framed a collage of the portraits from their milestones, such as the ones from their engagement party and Niagara Falls wedding. From there, it chronicled the precious shots of them cradling their two granddaughters as infants. The oldest, Anna Marie, was born three months before they married, but she always called her Grandma Mabel. Gregory and Rebecca stayed in Texas, but their regular visits allowed her to experience the joys of having children. She never regarded the girls as anything but her own grandkids.

With her permission, they also displayed the basket that held hers and Roy's mementos. She bought it the day after they reconciled, wanting to give their keepsakes the honor she bestowed upon those she had with Clark. To her delight, she acquired enough to fill it to the brim and placed the surplus in a desk drawer at home. Roy griped about her hoarding what he termed *junk* after a while, but every so often, she would catch him leafing through them.

Bev darted off to the kitchen to get the knife and forks for the cake-cutting, leaving her to muse alone. She cast her attention to the letters they laid on top of the basket, which she'd chosen. With one being a note she wrote to him and the other his message to her, she picked up the latter, which set their life together in motion. In easy and difficult occasions, his touching expressions fortified her love for him, like they did when she first read them on his porch.

Mabel,

I've berated myself over and over again for my lapse in reason and for what I said when we last spoke. I resent my foolishness for pushing you to stop here, and I'm sorry for my indignant response after you refused.

When you didn't accept my proposal, I strived not to show how much it hurt me, and I've done my best to mask my pain over being so far away from you ever since. I appreciate our calls and letters, but they always end too soon. After hearing about your struggles to have a child last week, I hung up the phone and cried because I wanted to hold you in my arms and soothe your heartache. At the same time, my love and esteem for you grew that much more. I'm in awe of the happiness you exude in spite of the troubles you've encountered.

I love your strength and realize you've had to develop a lot of it alone. I understand it's part of what makes you shy away from relying on others. I'll try not to play your hero unless I'm certain you want me to be. I want you to stay as you are and don't wish to hinder that.

If you can forgive me, I promise not to pressure you about anything, including our future. As much as I want us to be together, I can't lose you for good. I'll wait to marry you until I retire and can move there, but I won't force you if you aren't ready even then. Love comes from way down deep and never dies if it's really there. I'm convinced you and I share that, so time's

passing gives us nothing to fear.
  All My Heart,
  Roy

She set it down and dabbed away a tear, thankful to have found that love several times throughout her eighty-two years. She first experienced it with her parents, then Clark, and Evelyn, too. They'd been gone for decades, but the love that bound them couldn't be extinguished.

That fact eased her anxieties in facing the future as she watched her beloved husband's health deteriorate and grappled with her own loss of vitality. She observed him marching toward her with his cane, the *Happy Anniversary* banner hanging above him. She wondered how many more of them they'd celebrate together. The thought saddened her, but she dismissed it. Their love would live on like the others.

Roy whisked the letter out of her hands the instant he made it to her. "Are you reading that nonsense again?"

"This nonsense is what's given you forty years of wedded bliss, Mr. Stentz."

"Don't remind me." He winked and gave her a peck on the cheek. "Anna Marie insists we call her from here since she couldn't come, so I reckon we ought to before they make us cut the cake. I'll let you dial."

She took the cell phone they hardly used from him. "Why? You know I'm not any more reliable with this than I was when I transferred you to the steel factory."

He gave her the smile she so cherished. "What can I say? I enjoy the suspense!"

A word about the author…

Karina Bartow grew up and still lives in Northern Ohio. Though born with Cerebral Palsy, she's never allowed her disability to define her. Rather, she's used her experiences to breathe life into strong-minded characters who don't allow obstacles to stand in the way of the life they want.

Her past works include *Husband in Hiding*, *Forgetting My Way Back to You*, and *Brother of Interest*. She may only be able to type with one hand, but she writes with her whole heart!

www.KarinaBartow.com